REBEL
AT THE
END OF TIME

Steve Aylett is the author of *Slaughtermatic*,
LINT, *The Complete Accomplice*, *Rebel at the End
of Time*, *Toxicology*, *The Inflatable Volunteer*,
Atom, *the Tao Te Jinx*, *The Crime Studio*,
Bigot Hall, *Shamanspace*, *And Your Point Is?*,
Smithereens and *Novahead*.

ALSO FROM SCAR GARDEN PRESS:

NOVAHEAD
THE COMPLETE ACCOMPLICE
FAIN THE SORCERER
SMITHEREENS

SCAR GARDEN Kindle editions include:
FAIN THE SORCERER
NOVAHEAD
SLAUGHTERMATIC
REBEL AT THE END OF TIME
SHAMANSPACE
TOXICOLOGY
ATOM
SMITHEREENS

REBEL
AT THE
END OF TIME

STEVE AYLETT

Thanks to Mike Moorcock

REBEL AT THE END OF TIME by Steve Aylett

Completed in early 2007, first published in print 2011 by PS Publishing (UK)
copyright © Steve Aylett 2011

Scar Garden edition 2012

Cover artwork by Mo Ali

ISBN: 978-0-9565677-4-1

scargardenmedia@yahoo.co.uk

www.steveaylett.com

SCAR GARDEN PRESS — ALL STEVE AYLETT, ALL THE BLOODY TIME

"Power keeps hacking away at the weeds,
but it can't pull out the roots
without threatening itself"
– Eduardo Galeano

1

IN THE GOLDEN AGE

In Which the Duke of Queens Creates a Scene

Regina Sparks flew over a lion-coloured desert in a monoplane of clear glass. Birthing from the horizon was a pyramid of fitted gold, confetti crowds already gathering about it. She viewed the landscape through large jet eyes without whites. Her friends looked like a scattering of paste jewels.

The glass cross drifted to hover over the crowd, turning slowly. Regina's large black mouth curved into a smile as faces turned up to her. She flipped the plane sideways, settling it softly on the rise of a dune. Remembering to cease the engine sound and the spinning of the 'propeller', as she had learned to call it, she stepped down from the replica craft. She was an elfin negative of snow-white skin patterned with black tattoos of twisted vines. Her bare feet padded through roasted sand.

As she looked for the Duke of Queens, the guardian to whom she was so devoted, Regina spotted Bishop Castle's huge headdress swaying above the crowd. He was soon lost amid posturing gallants and beaked babies. The party was a throng of snouts, wings and tails. Here was a living totem pole of sullen expressions, there a large fleshy dice with a smile on each side.

Though free to choose their form by whim, caprice or professed philosophy, the oldest among Regina's neighbours chose to be human, with only minor variations. Some still trailed fashions which were almost spent: coloured shadows, bone companions, magnified heads and the 'hell' word used without context. What would replace these was yet to be seen – perhaps today a new notion would strike them all as fresh, or at least as something they hadn't tried for the last thousand years. It was often necessary, at the End of Time, to have a short memory.

The Iron Orchid emerged from the crowd like a ship's figurehead from a mist, resplendent in a dress of bacon, marmalade and black satin. 'Lady Miss Zebra,' she said, 'no party of the Duke's is complete without your two-tone presence.'

Regina smiled. 'As you can see, sweet Orchid, I've changed my patterning – stripes are tired, I now favour these lively vines, you see?' She turned once around, twisting her head to admire her own inked nakedness.

'So you do, Regina. Does it taste the same?'

'I don't know.'

The Iron Orchid bent to lick at Regina's breast. 'Cinnamon, ashes and human flesh.'

'Good?'

'Exquisite, my heart.'

'Is that your Napoleon?' Regina asked the Orchid, gesturing to a short fellow in a crimson uniform. The man took one bite from a cupcake and then hurled it to the floor, shouting at the sky with declamatory gestures.

'Yes,' said the Orchid. 'The most voluble of the three in my collection, I think. He weeps sometimes, for his lost empire.'

'He is possibly the real one?'

'Perhaps. He believes so, of course. I keep them in separate sections of my menagerie.'

Whisper Terrible floated down on a chicken-shaped weathervane which he straddled like a fairground horse. Landing, he dismounted the metal silhouette. Before they could go to greet him, Doctor Volospion strode over to them followed by a bone companion. The saturnine Doctor had conceded nothing to the theme and posed in his customary blue and purple brocade gown. 'Welcome, permanent bloom, and most white shade of pale. I look forward to the Duke's new extravaganza. What will he dream up next, I wonder?'

Though the Duke of Queens was universally admired for the scope and originality of his invention, it was generally acknowledged that he overdid things in terms of monumentalism. His scenes were also regarded as being somewhat impersonal and static: mere spectacle. Regina felt obliged to go to her guardian's defense. 'Uncle is throwing himself heart and body into this spectacle, Doctor Volospion. He has been about it several weeks in historical research.'

'I have seen pyramids before, somewhere.'

'Do you know what they are for?'

'Being tall,' he said vaguely, turning to gesture at the monolith, 'like that. And pointed. Perhaps pointing up at something in the sky.'

'It was more in the manner of a machine,' Regina

told him. 'For processing the death of kings.'

'Kings?' Volospion's sharp features became sardonic. 'A try at immortality, then, through a grand building project. Their methods clearly didn't work. I can't remember the name of a single king.'

Volospion's bone companion leant in at his shoulder and whispered, 'This too shall pass. And remember you are butter, man.'

'I'm getting a bit sick of these,' Volospion muttered, and touched a purple power ring on his left hand. The skeleton evaporated.

'Let us wait to see what the Duke has created for us,' said the Iron Orchid. She was being kind to Regina. 'The pyramid is impressive. And precise.'

'You are right, Madame Orchid,' Volospion conceded. He always looked rather stiff and uncomfortable when doing so. 'Let us wait and see.'

They walked through the crowds toward the pyramid base. Guests were still arriving – one in an air barge shaped like a swordfish, another in a basket under a balloon done up like an eyeball, and yet another rode in upon a giant haltered crab, the clacking claws of which caused alarm and laughter. Some dispensed with the illusion of requiring a vehicle and flew in without one, or blew in as a vapour and reconstituted with a small sonic thump. The Iron Orchid's son, Jherek Carnelian, arrived in a palatial river boat with a big turning side-wheel, a steam funnel, picket fencing and its own ghostly river which tapered out a few yards behind it. The floating palace drew cheers from the assembly. 'He learned about these things from Krill,' said the Iron Orchid, watching the strange craft, 'but I can scarcely believe such ... "zippy steamboats" really existed. Not in so elaborate a form.'

'Yet by rights the bumblebee should not be able to carry its own weight,' commented Volospion, pointing to the whale-sized bumblebee which was carrying Pastor Bulbous in to land. 'I suspect we are not equipped to judge the physics of the past.'

Jherek, startling in a suit of white duck, plus white hair and whiskers, walked down a ramp and announced ceremonially, 'Dang my buttons if I aint editor o' this barge!' He was immediately surrounded by chattering admirers. Regina wondered when she and Jherek would make love again, or have a long conversation. He was so busy with projects, such as his search in the old cities for platters of ancient cow-eating songs. She sighed and resolved to move on.

As Regina, the Iron Orchid and Doctor Volospion approached the base of the pyramid steps, they were joined by Lord Jagged of Canaria, resplendent in a cloak of gold leaf decorated with the repeated image of a beetle. Atop his pale head he wore a gold pyramid in honour of the Duke's theme. On Jagged it managed to look stylish.

'And what is the significance of this pest pictured on your cloak, Jagged?' Volospion asked immediately. He had long put himself in competition with Jagged, and that Jagged appeared oblivious to the contest irritated Volospion the more. 'Some obscure jest or reference you ache to spring directly into our faces?'

'Oh, the scarab, you know,' said Jagged, pirouetting a hand in the air, '... in honour of the theme.'

Their silence signalled that nobody knew the connection, and it seemed to Regina that Jagged seemed momentarily fazed.

'I speculate,' he told them, and returned to his usual assurance. 'I symbolise. The desert, dryness, this massive casing for the flying spirit of the dead. I chose an image I felt distilled these matters.'

'Since it requires explanation,' stated Volospion, 'it clearly fails to do so.'

'You are right,' Jagged said, with a slight bow. 'It is obscure.'

Volospion did not seem soothed by Jagged's easy surrender, but they were all distracted by the discovery of a table laden with bowls of bone shingle, popcorn, forest manna, blueberry pies, mutton saddles, starfails, canvasback ducks, head milk, lipstick, mako wine, black umbrella tea, galore bulbs, calories, sea grapes, compass cake, creme broulee, chrysolites, chains, quinces, bliss tongues, pandora flan, blushed snow, planetnut, amps, coleslaw, flame curd, matamata soup, anleesh, ebon root, pink lemons, skate, flaming puzzlash, sugar moss, pearl tails, ginger, plutonium, cloudberries, wing stew, skedaddles, salt, sevens, meatloaf, weasel coffee, turnovers, almanacs, gapdog, neverlegs and barley. 'No flying fish?' asked Regina.

'Too much trouble,' Lord Jagged said.

'You can weight them with anchors.'

'The planetnut is very good,' called Bishop Castle, who stood nearby. 'It goes pop in your mouth like a good curse.' He picked at his crenellated teeth.

'Argonheart has outdone himself,' declared the

Iron Orchid. 'Where is he?'

'He left in shame,' Lord Jagged told her, 'claiming the spread is a disappointment – a varied jumble without focus or theme.'

Whisper Terrible listened from the other side of the table. He had a sort of narrow bird head which ticked this way and that as remarks caught his attention.

'Such is life,' said Doctor Volospion.

'Is it?' asked Jagged without weight or emphasis. 'In any case, for Argonheart Po a meal is art, not life.'

'So it is for us all,' called Bishop Castle. 'Do any of us actually *need* to eat? I can't remember.'

'I recall going several decades without food,' Volospion said. 'I simply adjusted myself regularly, and made sure I was all there. Yes, food is art. And the spread before us does lack focus. Argonheart Po has earned his shame.'

'Perhaps he wished to feel it?' Regina suggested. 'The shame?'

'If so,' said Volospion, 'he went about it the right way.'

'He's a perfectionist,' shouted Bishop Castle. 'Try the smashed vampire crab, it's superb.'

Whisper Terrible spotted the trace of a skycloud which resembled an armchair, and flew away without flapping his thin arms, as though sucked up.

Revellers shared gossip as they milled before the golden slope of the pyramid. The sheer faces on either side of the broad central steps were of such a high polish that they held alchemised reflections of the guests, stretched and tapered toward the building's point. The Duke of Queens' features warped across this massive mirror as he floated up to Regina's group. He was resplendent in draperies of flaming ochre, and a pillbox hat of royal purple and Mars orange rested upon hair which was a tangle of gold wires. His sensitive face was transformed by eyes and teeth of mirrored metal. His spade-shaped beard, too, was a gilded mirror and the effect was striking.

'Uncle!' cried Regina, throwing her arms about his neck and kissing him so hard that his hat was knocked to a tilt. She backed up to admire his costume. 'It's perfect! Is everything prepared?'

'It is,' he smiled.

'Plans and stratagems, eh Duke?' said Lord Jagged amiably. 'This triangular castle is a fine backdrop.'

'Far more than that, my friend,' the Duke replied mysteriously. 'Ah, I see you have adopted the sign of the scarab – most appropriate.'

Bishop Castle yelled from the buffet. 'It's some sort of pagoda. But it's all filled in solid, Duke – with that golden stuff. What's it for?'

'Your question is a good one, oh crossed gamepiece,' replied the Duke, then spoke in a more level tone for Regina's group. 'This ridiculously large tapered thing behind me is a pyramid, a sort of storeyed shrine, part of the ancient Ass Tech culture which Principal Krill and Brannart Morphail agree occurred before the age of the Bird Reich and the Kali Yuga, more or less.'

'Krill and Morphail agree on so little, it must be true,' remarked the Iron Orchid, flicking a stellate snow spider from her shoulder. 'Don't you think that's a good sign, Lord Jagged?'

'It may be,' nodded Jagged without emphasis.

'So this raiment I'm wearing,' the Duke went on, 'is that of a king from a time of empire, all culpable in glory. Li Pao explained some of it, and also helped to compose my speech. What did he say about it?' The Duke was thoughtful. 'Ah yes, he said that there were flaws built in to the civilization – to make it more interesting I suppose. Apparently expansive, it was really a creature belted and restrained from its natural shape. And they felt they could make amends by a sort of ritual blood magic. They would kill the king.'

'Are you sure they killed the king?' Jagged asked mildly.

'Well it would hardly make sense the other way around, would it? The king would be killed as a suitable offering to the gods. I intend to immerse myself fully in the part.'

'I don't understand,' said Volospion somewhat irritably. 'Is this to be a lecture?'

'Far from it,' said the Duke excitedly. 'I will perform what was once known as a "sacraface". I am ritually killed upon the summit of this pyramid of mine, then conveyed downward into a coughing chamber within, and a gigantic golden replica of my face emerges from the front of the building. This sacred face makes the surrounding land fertile, a jungle grows up around the edifice, and the entire scene becomes the stuff of legend.'

'I am sure you hope it will be so, Duke,' muttered Volospion.

'Oh now, don't scoff, Volospion,' said the Iron

Orchid, throwing him a slight frown. Then she beamed kindly at the Duke of Queens. 'I find the Duke's "sacraface" most compelling. Perhaps finally we will all follow the fashion and be dead in gold, one and all.'

'One of us should remain alive to resurrect the rest, my hardest of perennials,' mentioned Lord Jagged.

'Ah! Of course. Well, Mongrove never participates. He'll notice our absence eventually.'

'You are to set a fashion, Uncle,' Regina whispered to the Duke, who smiled broadly.

But Lord Volospion had overheard. 'Yes indeed, Duke,' he remarked. 'I'm sure there has never been a more entertaining way of lacking inspiration.'

'What?' The Duke was confused.

'Ignore him, Duke,' said the Iron Orchid, who felt Volospion had finally crossed the line. She looked the Doctor in the eye. 'The Doctor is still smarting from his own recent project, merely.'

She was alluding to Volospion's creation of a village of live people made from pellucidant jade. The entire population of this glassy hamlet had immediately set about the Doctor with scorching volleys of sarcasm, none of which he had understood. He had turned to Lord Jagged to transcribe their ripe revelations, thinking to show off his grand creation in the process. When Jagged explained some of the puppets' arcane terminology, Volospion's humiliation was complete.

'I stated only what was on my mind,' he said now to the Iron Orchid, and then turned to the Duke of Queens. 'But, my apologies, Duke. I am sure you understand the frustrations which attend creativity, from time to time.'

Baffled, the Duke gave a slight bow. 'Indeed. Well, friends, I go to prepare. As should you all,' he added dramatically, and then swept away, disappearing behind a far corner of the golden edifice.

At his explanation of the pyramid scheme, the party-goers speculated that he was trying for a new subtlety. 'Compared to his pre-Kali Yuga New York this "pyramid" is quite small,' the Iron Orchid muttered to Regina. 'Perhaps a fifth of a mile high?'

Regina nodded.

'And he has taken the criticism of impersonality quite literally in the notion of absorbing himself into the structure. Am I correct?'

'I will merely say that my regal guardian has planned several weeks toward this spectacle,' Regina told her. 'He has spent much of that time in Principal Krill's Silence, deep in research. Did you see him, as excited as a boy – as excited as I have seen your son Jherek become before hosting a party. It is good to see my dear Duke so taken up.'

'His tendency to architectural gigantism may have changed,' stated Doctor Volospion, 'but his attire is still as gaudy as a rocket crab.'

'Come, my dear.' The Iron Orchid steered Regina away from the group. 'Let us stand by the fizzing well.'

She breasted forward like a Faberge galleon, leading Regina to the stained glass well in which bioluminescent portions of jigsaw puzzle flushed and flitted like fish. The Orchid glanced back to see that she and Regina had not been followed. 'Doctor

Volospion is doing his best, but is more competitive than usual for reasons I do not at present understand. I'm sure your sensitive guardian's party will be a spurting success.'

'And there is a part in it for me.'

'Really?'

'I am to perform the sacraface upon him, with a ... a .... Well, one of these.' She twisted her power ring and a broad swathe of flashing anzac metal swelled in her hand.

'A giant knife?'

'Yes. There is a more glamorous word, but I have forgotten it. See how sharp? I push that end into his belly and catch some of the juices in a bowl. There are some words I must say, and then he goes down into the pyramid. It will be very touching.'

'How long does he wish us to leave him dead?'

They were interrupted by a few sky valves which floated by, bloviating tunelessly. The two women were set to gazing aimlessly around the gathering.

A man passed in front of the sliming frame, a scintillating golden scaffold which dripped permanently with vinyl blood. To Regina's eyes accelerated colours instantly branded the stranger against the scene. She would later think he had appeared at the Duke's party as if signalling her. This was how things began to be changed.

2

THE RESCUE

Containing a Misunderstanding and an Execution

His hair and stubble pronounced the contours of his face like a martial helm, and in this form his face advertised itself as a living icon. Its combined wildness and symmetry suggested fiercely directed power. Wearing a red snakefruit jacket and purple leather pants, he was intently examining the very air around him. An occasional look of appalled disgust flinched across his face as he stalked through the crowds. He seemed to be his own shadow, a thing of brooding, brewing rage.

The Iron Orchid regarded the phenomenon in blank astonishment. This did not accord atall with the customary scattering of stancing lordalikes, pullulating aliens and fashionable phantoms which composed society at time's end. 'Who is that?' she asked.

'I don't know,' said Regina.

'Perhaps it is Fox Grave in a new guise. He likes to present himself as a man of bottled temper. His sky cutter is anchored near the mountains.'

'No, Fox Grave is over there.'

The pirate Fox Grave was still looking for the treasure he buried several million years ago, its sentimental value increasing with each millennium. Today he had made his lower body into clear glass and was passing spirals of fire through it for no good reason. He peered out at them through the bars of an espaliered collar as they looked his way, then began to negotiate the eating of a sandwich.

'Someone new, then?' Regina wondered aloud, as she turned back to the angry young man. The stranger was staring at the scrolled horns of Baron Coma. The Baron was sipping green rose wine and chatting affably with Again the Shuttle Clue, who had a thin stick projecting from his neck from which his head swung like a censer. The stranger ran a hand across the lime gold brocade of Coma's robe, and then turned to look directly at Regina Sparks. She felt a cellular chill flush down from her head to her toes.

Then he was gone into the crowd. 'I believe I shall go and find out,' murmured the Iron Orchid distractedly, wandering off after him.

When Regina turned, the stranger was standing next to her, his eyes flickering over her body of platinum black and China white, and away. 'So they keep their concubines naked,' he said. 'Terrible.'

'Concubine?' She looked directly at him, trying to catch his wandering gaze. 'Is that like a hedge-pig?'

He met her eye. 'It's natural to deny you're owned. The halter is not about your neck but in your mind, where it may be more effective. The invisible steel of oppression -' He was shoved by the gaster of a giant beetle as it chugged by behind him, but recovered quickly. 'This facsimile of joy is mere thoughtlessness, in inventive costume.'

'How do you conclude we are thoughtless?'

'By the amount of talk.'

'"Celebration has golden teeth,"' Regina quoted happily from somewhere.

'Such gaudy celebration usually denotes the fortune and freedom of all or the wielding of disproportionate power by a few.'

'I cannot say.'

'You cannot speak?'

Regina was bewildered. He was enflamed by something invisible to her.

'You are under duress?' He leaned in to her, urgent and confidential. 'You can trust me. Do you wish to be liberated? I can help you. Say the word.'

'Which particular one? I don't understand.'

'This is not a jest.' He looked around cautiously and lowered his voice further. 'Do you recognise me? Does anyone? Where is here?'

'You're on the tip of my tongue. Are you a new jester?'

He replied as if he had been carrying the response ready in his pocket: 'A court dance is the colour of favours in motion. Empires fall steadily, while outwardly they seem strong. Just as dawn comes steadily, not in surges. Not till the last.'

The remark had no familiar content. Was it a sort of password? 'Would you care to amplify?'

The stranger looked confused, and repeated all four sentences at deafening volume. Then with a startled look he slipped quickly aside into the crowd as Baron Coma hulked over. Regina and the Baron looked about for him. 'Who was that fellow?' Coma asked, lowering his rhinoid head.

Regina absently stroked his head-crest. 'He talked to me a great deal about how we all talk too much.'

'He appeared almost to have a beard. I wanted to question him about the precise mechanism of the thing. I fancy myself with two or three beards, one on my snout and one on each shoulder. Ah well, perhaps later.'

She still gazed off into the milling assembly, wondering if some invisible transaction had taken place. 'He seemed ... *serious*.'

Minutes later the Duke of Queens appeared at the summit of the pyramid, lights summoning around him and an air lens magnifying his figure like a screen. The warm wind knocked his robes. 'My people!' he proclaimed, and received a cheer. Some of the crowd levitated to better view the scene, which was clearly to be highly theatrical.

'Here we go,' said Volospion, looking up. The Duke did cut a fine figure against the chemical sky.

'You are my subjects,' the Duke announced, setting up the *dramatis personae*. 'By which I mean, my slaves. Do not dodge my meaning in search of comfort. I mean that you are less important than I, and worthless. Here I have given you a certain, though perhaps incomplete, definition of pyramidal society which may nevertheless prove to be very useful in practice if one is willing to act. The still force of regal scorn is granted by others – by you. This was once known as "zero point energy". To thank you for your perpetual donation would be to expose the fact, but still you would do nothing to correct it. For years I have believed you to be lacking enough moral power to take a resolution of any sort, while aware that the resolve forced by desperation may sometimes be the right one.' He spread his arms in generosity. 'It seems I alone am left to act. Let this be an example!'

Regina leant to the Iron Orchid's ear and whispered. 'I have my part to play.' And walking toward the pyramid ramp, she spread her arms, from which descended two curtains of scarlet gold in patterns of feathers. A scrolled cape sprouted from her shoulderblades and formed a train as she walked up the grand flight. Her sudden decoration drew gasps from the crowd, as it was rare that her monochrome body bore anything but inked designs and power rings.

'It's a drama!' Bishop Castle trilled. 'A ... a situation! Does anyone know what it's called, this sort of thing?'

The Iron Orchid frowned. 'I think ... an arbitration?'

'What "the hell" is it, my dear Duke?' called Bishop Castle.

'I think it's a prelude, merely,' Lord Jagged opined. 'To violence, perhaps.'

Volospion had an expression of raw wonder on his face.

Regina Sparks had arrived at the platform atop the edifice. Standing beside the Duke, she turned to face the crowd. She held a prodigious scimitar in her upturned palms like a platter.

'This tender young thing will provide the sacraface my empire demands!' shouted the Duke impressively, his gilt face flashing in the sun.

The Duke and Regina turned to face one another.

'Don't be afraid, my dear,' said the Duke, with a small nod.

The tide of guests parted at the base of the pyramid as a roaring machine cut through them and mounted the grand stairs. It was a twist of mechanism on two broad wheels, ridden by the stranger in the snakefruit jacket. He was leaning forward as if the machine could not move fast enough. At the summit he flew through the air between Regina and the Duke, skidding to a halt behind them and dismounting to stride forward.

'What's this about?' asked the Duke.

The stranger snatched the sword from Regina and held it aloft. He seemed intoxicated with outrage. 'With freedom comes responsibility,' he bellowed. 'And since we are not free, we act irresponsibly. Yet our masters feign shock and disappointment. Be proud of me now – I take full responsibility for this!'

And he plunged the sword into the Duke's stomach.

The Duke groaned, sinking to the stone ground. The stranger grabbed the dazed Regina and swung her on to his machine, mounting it behind her and riding off down the rear slope of the pyramid. They buzzed away across the desert, expelling a trail of smoke.

The crowd went wild.

3

FIRST IMPRESSIONS

In Which Doctor Volospion Lays a Wager

As a panel in the summit platform lowered the Duke's body into the building's mysterious depths, Volospion swatted his awe like a fly. A number of onlookers converged to compare notes on the spectacle.

'It was a completely ordinary tragic death, so what?' said Baron Coma. 'His life falling apart suddenly, there on the summit of his creation. He plunged in classic mode.'

'Exactly,' said Volospion, relieved at the negative opinion.

'I observed it too,' boomed Bishop Castle. 'And feel impressed.'

'Really?' the Baron frowned under the shadow of his heavy horns. 'You think I approached the event with a closed mind?'

'Not you, antlered one. You are merely distracted, I'm certain, by all that inventive cranial horseplay of yours.'

'I confess its endless permutations keep my thoughts constantly occupied. You have diagnosed the problem exactly. I failed to absorb the full impact of the Duke's show because of it. Of course, the fellow with the clown car was an unexpected touch. Yes, some drama there.'

'It was a motorized cycle, Baron,' Lord Jagged informed him.

'Murder wasn't it, the bit at the end? A marvelous effect!'

'I can't imagine how it would matter,' said Volospion mildly, swirling a goblet of chameleon vodka. 'It's no great departure from his sailing across one of Argonheart's giant puddings a few years ago. Or the time he sat there with, what was it, "scarlet fever"?'

'This was far more sophisticated, Doctor, as well you know.' The Iron Orchid swiped him playfully with a fan. 'And that wordy tantrum was redolent of history.'

'Which?' asked Bishop Castle, gathering more nibbles onto a plate. 'The Duke's or the boy's?'

'Well, both.'

'And just what the party needed,' added Lord Jagged, thoughtfully. 'Substance. Texture. But the surprise twist was the thing.'

'How do you mean, my brightest canary?' asked the Orchid.

'The interloper. You see, he's done something quite clever, the Duke. A spectacle or vision is momentary. The value of it does not really survive the moment in which it was new. A *story*, however, such as the one the Duke has set in motion, goes forth and weaves itself among us all. It is participatory, ongoing, and even perhaps meaningful.'

'Oh, really, Lord Jagged,' Baron Coma scoffed. Jagged had gone too far. '*What* does it mean?'

'I haven't the slightest idea, Baron – perhaps

merely that we should all have giant golden faces.'

'I've had a hankering for a larger face,' said Castle from the buffet. 'Not made of gold, though. Glass, perhaps.' The fashion for glass was tailing off but Castle was yet to know it.

Lord Jagged of Canaria was warming to his own theory and had become a centre of attention. 'It's clear the Duke constructed this drama at length – it explains his weeks of absence. Not even he could spend such a time dreaming up a mere entombment in a triangular house. The scene continues with the abduction of his ward and whatever happens between them. The Duke is attempting a ... a moral, d'you see?'

'Meaning or moral, what is it?'

'Well I don't know, Doctor, but that will doubtless become clear. That's in the nature of a story, as opposed to the sort of instant spectacle we are accustomed to. Yes, I do believe the Duke is finally working to outdo us all. And certainly he should not be reconstituted at this time!'

'But why ever not?' asked the Orchid. 'We need him to explain himself.'

'Can't you see, my dear Orchid, that this latest death of his is part of the dramatic tale he planned so carefully? Do you want to spoil that tale before its denouement? The Duke would be terribly upset!'

'Of course! After all his work. As usual, Lord Jagged, you see the situation in all its detail, and with all its social ramifications tilting this way and that like hammerflowers. Shall we put him in some snow, for now?'

'I think he's just sunk into the famous "coughing chamber" he spent so long telling us about,' Volospion pointed out. 'That part at least went off as he intended, don't you think, Jagged?'

'I feel certain it has,' said Jagged, struck by the notion. 'That must be a very important part of the drama. Oh, how pleased the Duke will be when we resurrect him at his story's conclusion and he sees we have understood and acted along precisely as he intended!'

Volospion decided to state his case. 'I am not convinced the scene we witnessed accorded entirely to the Duke's plan.'

'Whatever do you mean?' asked the Iron Orchid.

'Precisely what I say. That we may have witnessed an intersection of script and chance.'

'It is true that one's creations do not always attend to one's wishes,' Jagged remarked with no hint of a double meaning.

Volospion drew himself up. 'Have you heard, sir, of the term "wager"?'

'I'm not sure.'

'Aha! A "wager", my dear Lord of Canaria, is an elaborate journey of chance and regret.'

'Regret?'

'Another ancient term. Yes, I know it's complicated. You see, so many of these antique concepts are dependent on ... lack. A finite amount of things, you see? Acts and decisions which cannot be undone, that's the point of it. Well, we can't reproduce such ludicrous conditions here, except in regard to the expenditure of time, which is supposedly receding into short supply.'

'You still don't believe it, Doctor Volospion?'

'I have yet to see undeniable evidence. But the point I labour to make, Lord Jagged, is that we may salvage a crumb of peril from the past, via my "wager". I contend that the Duke's show went awry, with that young interloper being a random bit of chaos. You contend that it was staged and plotted as an extension of the theme. Whichever of us is right owes a forfeit or favour to the other.'

'What will the forfeit be?'

Volospion had not thought this far. He pondered, and was suddenly illuminated. 'If the angry fellow in the spiky jacket is accidental and unplanned, I take him for my menagerie.'

'And if he is a mere phlizz created by the Duke?'

'Then you take it for yours,' said Volospion, amused. 'I believe it is customary to throw a heavy glass bust of Napoleon into a blast furnace upon agreeing a wager. But we can forego it.'

'A wager! I'll participate,' said Bishop Castle, licking his fingers, 'if a similar buffet is provided.' He bit some flesh from a chicken drummer and threw the chog over his shoulder. It bounced off the skull of his bone companion and the Bishop gave an impatient sigh, demolishing the walking skeleton with a twist of a power ring. The change in fashion was instantly contagious – bone companions exploded to dust throughout the gathering.

'Rich farewell to dry company,' hailed Baron Coma, and rode away on two glum-looking horses, one of which was mounted and copulating upon the other.

'He's got that wrong,' Volospion confided to the Iron Orchid. 'Those things are called palindromes – they're meant to have a head at each end.'

'Now, Doctor, how do we make sense of the Duke's intent?' Lord Jagged asked. 'We must if we are to resolve this flutter of yours.'

'*Wager*, Jagged,' Volospion corrected him, pleased at the opportunity for scorn.

'Principal Krill,' said the Iron Orchid. 'He helped the Duke with his research.'

'That mound of nostrils?' Volospion exclaimed. 'But, well, I suppose he does know more "history" than most of us. And I confess I respect his skill with wooden birds and furniture.'

'I haven't seen the birds. Are they good?'

'They do everything a – what was it? – a "meat" bird used to do. They fly, shout very concise bits of advice to people down on the ground, lay beautifully carved little eggs, and rot down to a delicate *wooden* skeleton!'

'Ah, that's art, you see, Volospion,' Jagged remarked. 'He's not all "history".'

'Oh I admit he has skill.'

The party was breaking up as they strolled toward one of the docking areas. A strange sound alerted them to the sight, far behind them, of Bishop Castle sucking the entire remaining fare from the table into a massively distended, fluming mouth. 'Will you join us, Bishop?' Jagged called, but received no response.

When they reached the landing field, Volospion piped up. 'We'll take my gaseous insect,' he told them. Towering behind him was a cherry glass mantis with a scarlet gas mask for a face. 'This is the *Mantis Malamatis*. It handles well – I think you'll be pleasantly surprised. It's red glass with a rubber mask, you see?'

'Does this use that ion wind idea you were talking about?' Jagged asked.

'I don't really know. It goes, anyway.'

'It's lovely, Doctor,' offered the Iron Orchid, as they walked up a thin wing to the entrance. 'Glass is with us for at least another day or so.'

The wings buzzed into pink motion and disappeared, the insect rising up and canting as its legs folded away. Soon the vehicle was flitting over a wasteland littered with fragments of purple flint. Seated inside, the three idly observed the bending landscape through the red lens around them.

Volospion was still wondering what material would replace glass, when the Iron Orchid made a striking remark.

'Doctor, your fine rigidity of view has at all times included a tempering rigidity of etiquette and manners.'

'Thank you, dear Orchid,' he replied, surprised.

'Yet I have noticed,' the Iron Orchid continued, 'today, a distinct increase in your level of, shall we say, inventive scorn.'

'Indeed?' Volospion said, and he needed only an instant's thought to see the truth of it. 'Well yes, now that you point it out I perceive I have been more caustic than usual. What is it, most rigid of blooms? Jagged, is something wrong with me? With my face and jaws?'

'Perhaps you are wanting for something,' suggested the Iron Orchid.

'How could I be? The very idea is fantastical.' He frowned. Had somebody re-animated some mind disease from the past? Was it a new jest? 'I shall have to think on this. In the meantime, friends, forgive me any untoward outbursts.'

'Perhaps you are deciding gradually to become a social disaster,' said the Orchid, looking outward at the plain, 'like Profumo the Monkey.'

'Perhaps, perhaps,' muttered Volospion distractedly.

4

A CURIOUS KRAKEN

Showing What Level of Illumination May Be Expected
When a Squid is Consulted

The clockwork detail of Krill's seashore Silence came into view. Its green dome swivelled like an owl's head, one big eye observing them. Volospion sent out a mental inquiry. 'May we enter, Principal Krill?' He received a glutinous assent and the mantis deployed its many legs, settling softly upon Krill's air jetty. The three disembarked and entered the Silence through a trapezoidal opening. As they descended through levels of lexicons, smudged portholes and silverine map tubes sealed with wax, Lord Jagged resumed his reasoning regarding the interloper. 'I wonder, Volospion, that you don't consider his speech.'

'A couple of transposed phrases abutted together,' Volospion declared. 'It was tedious.'

'He spoke our language – which would suggest he was the Duke's creation. Or had been given a translation pill by the Duke.'

'Or by someone else!'

'Not very likely, if he is the wild thing you assert.'

They smelt the mix of salt water, artificial age-dust and pickled knowledge that hung around Krill and his enthusiasms – Krill had found a way for damp and dust to co-exist without sludging – and entered his green silverine chamber. Mechanical cases held books bound in muscle, books which opened with a key, books thicker than they were wide and books rotten as fruit. In one corner stood a russet world globe like a giant conker tattooed with cryptic empires; behind this, prospering fungi had made a wall of skin shelves. On a small platform in the circular chamber's centre was a pile of draped tentacles crowned with a brain like a crumpled hat. Krill had presented this guise for so long that nobody, himself included, remembered if he was human, alien or artifice. Behind him a bay window thundered low with a sea of recent vintage, overlooking the crest of a fluorescent reef. Undersea animals like intestines touched the stained glass and moved on. A coil of eyes drifted amid palmate fronds in rich yellow, and a lovely grace note was a rose of suspended blood which roiled like a tornado above the reef. Volospion found it very tranquil and sinister. 'Greetings,' he said, 'prime pullulator.'

'Hail,' Jagged took up, 'tantacular tutor.'

'I bid you halloo,' said the Iron Orchid, 'oceanic expositor.'

A mouth tore open like a pocket, trailing rinds of green skin like seaweed. 'Welcome, eternal friends.'

As was customary, the visitors spent a brief time examining Krill's newest acquisitions. Jagged inspected an ancient platter player which could emit recorded sounds through a lily-shaped trumpet, and Volospion ran a hand over a square hull of blue shellac. His fingers were intercepted by one of Krill's remarkably fastidious limbs. 'This,' Krill remarked, 'is a radio, a form of shellfish. Its legs have not survived, but they went here.' The tentacle prodded at the four lower corners, then retreated like a wave.

A green mannequin with velvet hair and a lyre in one hand hung smiling from a cornice. The Orchid tapped its dangling foot. 'Is this one of Jack-in-the-Green's?'

'I expressed admiration and he gifted it me. It sings the future, or what is a mile away, or something like that.'

'Astonishing.'

'And these wooden roses on the furniture are designed to bloom and even pollinate. That's what this stuff is – not dust but chair pollen, do you see?'

Courtesies dispensed with, the visitors broached the subject of the Duke's party. 'We have been awakened by an astonishing intruder,' said Lord Jagged.

'What a thunderbolt!' added the Orchid.

'Show me,' Krill said. From the floor arose a skeletal clockwork table. 'The key fits right into the bone.' He wound the key in the table, and the three visitors' attention animated a scene of tiny figures which bubbled up from its surface. A tide of guests swarmed in around the Duke's golden pyramid, upon which the Duke stood and gave his complicated speech. Principal Krill listened closely, his blue-green and grey head valving like a heart. Regina Sparks stood beside the Duke, her monochrome body distinct in the tableau. And then a toy-sized rider sped up the slanted wall and delivered his peculiar pronouncement, which Krill paused and played a second time before allowing the scene to complete. The diorama closed down.

'Magisterial,' Krill declared. 'Eloquent.'

'And Bishop Castle was rigorously eating everything he saw,' Jagged added.

Krill flubbered a laugh. 'I like Bishop Castle.'

'We all do.'

'What do you make of the theme, Krill?' asked Volospion. 'You helped the Duke with research for it, after all.'

'He enquired after pyramidal tradition from the Ass Tech, Haninn and Tairona empires, but never told me how he planned to employ the knowledge. Perhaps he told Li Pao, whom he also consulted.'

'But what about the fellow on two wheels, and his talk of "responsibility"?' Volospion asked, trying for 'indignation'. 'What did it mean, all that? I feel indignant about it.'

Volospion himself had set the gold standard for meandering diatribes eight years earlier with his 'Turn Me Upon Myself' tirade. It had been the high watermark of the fashion and certain schullers, such as Principal Krill, had claimed to understand it. Krill had made second- and third-hand screeds by rearranging the words. 'Me Upon Myself Turn' and 'Turn Upon Me Myself' were judged the best by his polite if puzzled audience. But in private it was deemed to have become too specialized – perhaps even tedious – and Volospion had criticised Krill for merely rearranging his ideas. Krill had responded by introducing obscure words from his library, but 'Turn

Upon My Empathy' was scuppered by the realisation that Krill himself did not know the meaning of the new term. The fashion had knotted itself into complete inaccessibility. But the two-wheeled man seemed, improbably, to be saying something different.

'Mayhaps he was merely failing aloud,' the Iron Orchid suggested, her attention already wandering. She had no great love for Krill's dank quarters.

His 'indignation' offered and ignored, Volospion put it away, puzzled – he would try it again in different circumstances. He hadn't a clue what it was for, really. Enjoyment?

Krill's pulsatile bonce seemed thoughtful, several wet valves opening and closing in succession. Then he stated: 'The Duke of Queens was representing himself as the head of a government, possibly an empire. The two-wheeled man was, or was posing as, a revolutionary.'

'What exactly was a government?' asked the Orchid, and Krill explained.

'Indeed?' said Volospion, intrigued. 'Any pirate or madman would be entirely pleased to have even one in his collection.'

'Well, that's that,' said the Orchid briskly. 'Shall we go?'

'Wait!' Volospion halted her. 'There remains the matter of the "revolutionary".'

'Yes, Krill,' said Lord Jagged with a mild smile. 'Tell us what you know about our rambunctious raree.'

Krill's treacly eyes regarded the unflappable Lord Jagged. 'Rambunctious is he?'

'He's basically a fuselage with a snout.'

Krill stared a while more. Watching, Volospion supposed that Jagged had implied some doubt as to Krill's knowledge. But it was Krill who had introduced everyone to the fashion for bone companions after his researches into the wild frontier of the American West. His insistence that the skeletons wear coonskin caps was the clinching touch of authenticity.

Krill began his explanation. 'Fissure Science, the science of what has been left out, shows us that gaps in knowledge have a shape – a shape which can tell us a great deal about what should dwell there. Fetch me down that blue-gold triangular book, Volospion. *The Grimoire Yetneyet*. Rayskin binding, spine like an eel.'

Volospion wondered why Krill didn't reach for it himself with one of his arms – he had never previously missed an opportunity to be creepy and undulant – but obliged. He shook the book, and opened it. 'These pages won't mix.' He handed it to Krill.

'You consider this fact exceptional? It is not. If history teaches us nothing else it's that matters were fixed, for months or years at a time. Thank you. Now, observe – this page, and this. The information is packed in by a process of endlessly proliferating inverse contradictions. Unfortunately this means that there must be an equal number of false statements in it as there are true facts.'

'How do you tell the difference?' asked the Orchid.

'By trial and error. You may even contrast a couple of truths to reach a third. For instance: "Synergy – the behaviours of whole systems not predictable from the behaviours of the individual elements", and "Obviouswhynergy – the behaviours of individual elements not predictable from the behaviour of whole systems". Now, in reference to our party-crasher. Revolutionaries feel a need to explain their acts – dictators do not. You can even track the transition from one to the other in this need to be understood. It might be thought that you could measure the age of an institution by the number of times it has become its opposite while retaining its original name. But in practice, once an institution becomes its opposite, it remains so as long as profitable power can be wielded for it in that permutation. This may be one of the key themes of the Duke's drama, in fact.'

Lord Jagged of Canaria interjected with effortless precision: 'You believe, then, that the revolutionary is one of the Duke's cast of actors?'

'You know very well, Jagged,' Krill returned. 'Ahem … that I cannot yet say.'

'How did an empire respond to such revolutionaries?' the Orchid enquired. 'Could it cope?'

'Empire collapse can occur without revolution, according to history – being a matter of empire physics, troy equations and such. It's all based on energy expenditure, resource extension and principle drift, you see? Over-extension on top and loss of principle at the foundation. Revolution, depending on its effectiveness and honesty, can retard or hasten this collapse. As you can tell, I am equipped only to describe generalities.'

'Which are getting us nowhere!' cried Volospion. 'How to proceed?'

'If the young man is an alien, our dear Regina may be in actual danger!' the Iron Orchid marvelled. 'Imagine it!'

'I doubt any such anomaly will occur,' mused Lord Jagged. 'She has her power rings – I suspect she will enjoy the experience, whatever it is. But a course of action occurs to me. What if we spin up an "empire" for this fellow?'

'What do you mean?' Volospion asked.

'It is not a statement open to wide interpretation. I mean ...'

'He means for us to whip up an oppressive regime for a day or two!' the Iron Orchid exclaimed, seeing the idea.

Jagged's smile was strange. 'I believe this is what the Duke intends. To continue the drama he so carefully appointed. And in the process of interaction we may let our interloper prove himself as one thing or another.'

'I'll confess it has texture, Jagged,' Volospion admitted, surprised again at Jagged's angularity of thought. From where did he retrieve such notions? 'I have an ancient recording which could help with that. It tells of a real jewel-box of an empire. With a big smoky head.'

'We could put the courtiers in a deep pit,' the Orchid suggested.

'Set up tollgates,' added Jagged. 'And charge money.'

'Money?' asked Volospion, fluttering his hands as if to conjure the enigmatic concept.

Krill explained.

'I see – it immediately provides a means of issuing unthinkable orders to good men! I agree that we should play along, for the purpose of our wager. We will discover if the crazed youth's attack was choreographed or if there was anything accidental or authentic there atall.'

'Authentic?' said Lord Jagged, absently examining a fossilized phone. 'Kudos to the Duke if there were.'

Volospion ignored him. And reaching for their power rings they set about recreating, as far as their knowledge allowed, the structures of a past age. In this they were veterans since a time their own memories could not recall.

5

A GIRL FROM A DIFFERENT WORLD

Wherein the Stranger Begins to Sense His Mistake

They stopped in the Hapexian Wasteland. She walked a way from the vehicle and looked at the components at her feet. Here was strange debris, not one article of it alike to another. A million scenes had been made and demolished here, leaving these traces. The stranger followed her, taking off his jacket which was spiky like a fruit. He draped it over her shoulders, she didn't know why. She crouched down and tilled through some bits. A glass padlock containing a preserved scorpion, a lump of shocking pink coal, a feathered medal, a semi-transparent amber screw, a domino of green wood, a playing card which was perpetually burning. She showed him this last. 'Isn't it beautiful?'

He seemed baffled, groggy. He knelt next to her, picking things up. A cross-sectioned ammonite containing blue oil, a piece of ice in a green rubber cage, a black root studded with tiny white screaming faces, a small disk of olvis timber. Principal Krill had invented four new colours – olvis, cry, zild and severin – and was happy for anyone to use them.

The stranger stood with a sudden inbreath, looking to the sky. 'I don't know where I am. This place … maybe this is what happens.'

'Happens? When?'

'When you win. Maybe you get kicked up to another level like a videogame. It would explain a few things.' He glanced back at his vehicle. 'Motor's not even ticking down. So hot out here.'

She turned a silver power ring for a cool breeze, which he seemed to appreciate, closing his eyes.

'Is this all part of the plan?' she asked. 'You taking me?'

'I didn't rescue you by accident, if that's what you mean.'

'I thought for a moment the Duke would be upset.'

'He's quite incapable of being upset about anything, I assure you.'

'Ofcourse you're right – the dear. And it was a wonderful "rescue".'

'If only it would rain.'

Regina touched the blue power ring on her left hand and rain began falling. A black umbrella pumped open from her hand.

'How can you walk around like that – naked except for those tattoos?'

'It's easy.'

'It's shameless.'

He seemed galvanic with refusal. A multidirectional refusal, of everything perhaps. His beauty was like a bull eating a rose.

'I don't know what you mean. It's very authentic. Principal Krill says the earliest age of man was without colour, the black and white age. The technical term was *mono erectus*. Some theorize that that age was also entirely silent, and only later was there full colour and sound. Principal Krill has visual records of prehistory and it's quite true.'

'Your Principal Krill has a lot to answer for, it seems.'

'Oh, yes. He's given everyone so many ideas about the past. The visual records I mentioned also show that people moved very quickly then, with an almost jerky motion, like this -' She strutted this way and that, kicking up trinkets and wobbling her head. 'And laughing silently, like this.' She chuckled without sound, bobbing her head.

'Please stop. Stop. You have it wrong.'

'Not me. Brannart Morphail's research has supported the idea with the fact that black and white were kept separate for many millennia. Or did they alternate?' Regina stopped, struggling to remember. 'Atom and Ease were the first people and they were black. But when one of their sons killed the other, the killer turned so pale with bad feeling that he stayed white to the end of his days. All white people were children of the criminal. Later black and white mixed together. And finally everyone decided that millions of different colours would be more interesting to look at. The Pixel Age. What's your name?'

'I am Leo del Toro.'

'Leo del Toro, I am Regina Sparks of Queens Parish, how do you do?'

'I believe I am going mad.'

'I've tried it, it was fun.'

The stranger frowned, gazing slightly away. He looked almost frightened. A thread of rain was ticking off of his hair. Regina watched this awhile, then cancelled the rain. As the umbrella dissolved and blew away like smoke, Leo del Toro muttered 'Yesterday I stumbled; thus today I stand straighter than ever.' Then he turned to her with resolve. 'Regina,' he said. 'Perhaps you can help me. I don't know whether you understand – you may have been drugged. But those who sent you up the pyramid – they require justice. Governance is their cardinal virtue. How, then, will they ever atone for their sins?'

She thought at first he had departed from his appointed role. A proper look at his countenance, however, was enough to convince her of his absolute sincerity.

'No doubt they have others in captivity. Prisoners. Where are these slaves kept?'

Regina thought a while. 'There are menageries.'

'These "menageries" hold people? Human beings?'

'Well, for instance I know that the Iron Orchid has several old French people in hers. Because of their identity she keeps them apart of course.'

'And you see nothing wrong in this abomination?'

'It's the Orchid's affair.'

'Your mind is owned – I see you're like a child still. But I have the cure. Where are these menageries? Take me there.'

Regina called up the *Howland*, her glass monoplane, bubbling it out to accommodate a bay for Leo's vehicle.

'Sorcery!' he cried.

'Yes.'

*

She was surely mad. And allowed to pilot a plane?

'Hey, the steerin' will's got leopardskin fur! It's new!'

'Please be careful.'

'You're funny.'

He was seated in a transparent bubble behind her as the plane made a muted buzzing and slanted weirdly upward, a clumsy bracket with no detectable engine. He knew the wrongness of it all, the same way he could find, without thinking, every bullet and blade and torture scar on his body; every point to place explosives on a dam.

Less than a day ago, so far as he could tell, he had been racing away from the remnants of a police agency that had yet to accept the new order. Seconds after jettisoning a HERF cannon he had glimpsed a throbbing transparency ahead and felt momentarily submerged, alchemical lights bursting around him – the front wheel, the handlebars and his own gloved hands dissolving. A few instants of blackout and he found himself riding again, still chewing the nugget of pine pitch he'd popped into his mouth as he sped away from the celebrations. And he was riding through a landscape of colours richer than paint could sustain. It had an instant flavour of crowded, useless opulence. Amid the floors and hinges of a ruined utopia, working furnaces glowed cherry red. Leather snails the size of Volkswagons grazed on silver grass. In the distance stood palaces resembling Hawaiian drinks. From every direction elaborate aircraft and bucolic land barges converged on a far gilt pyramid.

'Re-jeena ...'

This hourglass slave, her topless heart benign but unbalanced. The girl whose skin was snow and ink, the only variation the varicoloured rings on her fingers. Apparently unaware of danger or degradation. She'd shown him a junkyard of apocalypse clutter – billions of partial, baffling trinkets. One of the components was fuzzy like a migraine blot. When he tried looking directly at it he'd seen a blank hole in his palm and felt the squirming of the mycelial tendrils at the back of his eyes as they tried to evade the approaching information.

All his polarities were deranged. For hours he had been moving half-conscious through tilted perceptions, trying to act well in a dream. Was it a psychotic break? He'd long been sick of his own atmosphere, but that was an irrelevance. Leo had years ago made a covenant with justice and was fully prepared for his life to end with a tawdry execution beside a jungle runway, once his victories had been forgotten by all but his enemies. He had fought a state that fitted its crimes together so perfectly they made a picture of unbroken honesty, supported by the ravening expediencies of media. He was incapable of self-pity; ruthless but not shameless; pragmatic. And in this alien feverscene he grasped at right action as at a life ring. Where was it?

They were skimming over a desert of lime-green sand. He saw a starshaped building below. 'There it is,' Regina called back to him, moving the joystick back and forth at random. The plane descended, hovering on the horizontal.

They landed near a mandalically intricate courtyard planted with mustard-mossed statues and an art deco greenhouse like a jukebox. Approaching this and peering in, Leo found it was crowded with winged roots and zebra orchids. He turned to find Regina's magnified eyes observing him.

'Lord Jagged says nature cannot be left to complete improvisation,' she said, and smiled. Fast black specks of brownian motion fizzed in her white skin. 'Only its broadest outline is not determined by our dreams.'

A set of keys landed on his leg – it was a stick bug, its four long wings like sycamore seeds. It instantly pushed off again, its spring exerting surprising force.

At the main building Leo grasped a doorhandle like an iron starfish and pushed in to a vast hallway with a red glass floor and walls of purple fish-scale tile. Regina led him to a central chamber from which several 'habitats' radiated, each viewable through a lancet window. Through the first of these Leo saw a man dressed as Napoleon, scrutinising a map upon a thick oaken table with fierce concentration. Through the next window Leo saw another Napoleon practicing his fencing. Through a third he saw Napoleon wearing frilly pantaloons and drinking wine: lethargy writ large.

'Obviously when you said "menagerie",' Leo stated, 'you meant "asylum". These creatures are deluded.'

'Not at all,' said Regina. 'One is real, the others are false, conjured up at various times. But they all believe themselves the original.'

'Like I said. Well, I guess I'd better release them

anyway. Stand back.' He wrenched a large red lever, doors retreating in a sudden plunge as the building transformed. The contracting architecture disgorged its captives into the central room, where the three Napoleons stared at one another in astonished affront. Then they set about attacking each other, the one with the foil showing a distinct advantage. None of this was so distracting that Leo failed to notice the jamboree of species ejected into the observation chamber with the same convulsion – a gaggle of fancy-dressed fools bent on larking about. One was dolled up as a dolphin.

Leo ran his fingers through his hair in annoyed confusion. 'Alright,' he demanded, 'what's it all about?'

Regina was looking about at the confusion. 'Oh I'm enchanted by trouble. It has such ... texture! And angles, such strange angles all at odds with one another!' In her enormous eyes was sky-wide astonishment.

Had he got it all wrong then? Had he died and landed himself in a jam? This girl with her skin of cracked and re-joined porcelain, was she an angel?

What if you met an angel and it didn't have anything original to say?

6
THE MASQUERADE
Consisting of Sundry Preparations for Governance

They had made a domed palace near Lord Jagged's cage-like castle on the red mesa, but weren't making much progress otherwise. There was a lot of activity in the main hall as new arrivals landed on the adjoining platform every few minutes and Principal Krill presided from a huge glass vat of water mounted on caterpillar tracks. They discussed the plan in detail, each detail scrambling away from every other like termites. 'Who shall play the part?' Doctor Volospion was asking.

'My Lady Charlotina is adept at gossip and social drama,' the portly Bishop Castle commented, drinking Syrian arak, 'but would she grasp the politics?'

'Who among us could?'

'Mistress Christia?' suggested Lord Jagged of Canaria. He had changed back into his customary outfit, a mass of quilted daffodil at the summit of which his head seemed besieged and reduced. His coat was parted at the rear to project a yellow swallowtail.

'Isn't it just a question of scale?' Volospion cut in. 'I mean in the number of other people affected? Imbalance, in fact.'

'Perhaps you're right,' said Jagged, unconvinced.

'Whoever assumes the role of leader,' bubbled Krill, 'will need advisers providing a constant series of prompts. Doubtless that's how it was done anyway. Artificial advantage is yet advantage. Anything can be contained within a carapace of proper procedure. It'll seem quite authentic. I had a look at Volospion's antique disk portraying such a scene and it's as he described it – a shouting head speaks the rules of the moment, but is controlled by a man behind a curtain. And a dog, I believe.'

'A dog?' Bishop Castle raised his voluminous red eyebrows. 'Were the views of dogs held in such high regard?'

'Perhaps it was a balancing technique – one opinion from the man of mind, and a balancing view from the animal of instinct.'

Lord Jagged made another dubious noise.

'I suppose we could take turns, so long as the external appearance is roughly consistent. But what exactly should this leader be like? How to play it?'

'Ominous! And ... coarse?'

'A stressed rascal, perhaps.'

'No, no – a gothic misfit!'

'A threadbare monster, vicious as a honey rat.'

'A twitching titan with wires attached which lead to his people, so with every convulsion his people must spasm and suffer?'

'Ridiculous.'

'Should it have gills, wings? Horns?'

'No,' stated Krill. 'It's important that you look human. Very. The masses were, historically, not wise enough to see that real villains are rather bland. Certainly no horns, no. Wings? No, I don't think so.'

'A cape, perhaps?' asked Bishop Castle. 'As a concession to the ... the tradition of it all?'

'Capes ... You know, I really have no idea.'

Bishop Castle looked glum.

'Oh a cape, why not?' Krill relented exuberantly. They both laughed.

'On a throne,' Jagged continued, 'trying to look entire. This is our chief error, in the stranger's eyes. There was a difference of levels, you see, between one person and another.'

'Levels?' the Iron Orchid asked. 'You mean they stood on different platforms at varying heights?'

'In a way, but these were levels which were accepted, er ... organised ... accepted, according to money. They called it class.'

'"If you want admirers, avoid equals",' Volospion chipped in.

'The trick was to create social conditions in which a man is maimed and limited by his honesty,' Krill explained. 'That shored up the levels.'

'Did folk not feel insulted at their freedoms being written by someone else?' asked Bishop Castle. 'Or was it a game?'

'The people in the government settled it amongst themselves,' stated the Orchid, somewhat redundantly. She looked rather lost.

'But,' muttered Bishop Castle to himself, visibly exerting his mind, 'the government was merely some more people.'

'And a military, with the threat that implied.

Those were also people, however,' said Krill. 'It probably seemed incongruous even at the time. And the government were, in some cases, elected.'

'Elected. How many people in a government?'

'Well, thousands.'

'All elected. I don't understand.'

'My friend, neither do I.'

'The military – these were entertainers?'

'No, my high-hatted fellow,' Jagged laughed fondly, 'they were a force of violence and threat. An overseer's permanent disapproval will tend to lose its charges' obedience, unless backed with force.'

'Ah.'

'You see?'

'No.'

The dwarfish scientist Brannart Morphail arrived, bouncing on his balls like a spacehopper. He shrank the balls and stood up.

'Brannart!' Jagged hailed him from the snugs of his tall lilac collar. 'What do you think? We whipped up the palace in a jiffy and are just sorting out the finer details of an ornamental tyrant. Everything shall legally flourish for our advancement. We will issue daily edicts stating what is to be "unimaginable". What do you make of the idea?'

'I suppose it might be impressive if revealed by flashes of lightning, but not otherwise.'

'Oh, and we were doing so well.'

'Brannart,' said Volospion. 'Decided against ears, old fellow?'

'These *are* my ears!' Morphail protested, grabbing his ears as if protecting them.

'Sorry, Brannart, didn't see them there.'

'Where should they be if not my head?' Morphail asked after Volospion, who was looking blandly away. '*Where?*'

'What's that on your back, Brannart?' Bishop Castle asked. It was rare for Morphail to adjust his hobbled form.

'Stone wings. Irony, you see?'

'I don't see how.'

'Well – wings. Made of stone. Opposite of what's required?'

'Is it?'

'Real wings were made of feathers, very light.'

'Were they?'

Morphail slumped. 'I'll get rid of them.'

'Sorry old fellow, went right over my head.'

'Is that a joke?'

'If you say so, old fellow.'

'The problem is we've a surfeit of irony, Brannart,' Lord Jagged offered, a kind smile on his linen-white face. 'You bring colds to Cowgate.'

'What are these?' Brannart asked, gesturing up at some long flags on the back wall.

'They are pennants, a witty word created to echo "penance", the shackling of oneself to an official burden – according to Krill's old history *Yetneyet*. Jherek devised the design.'

'That book expired years ago like a candle,' snapped Morphail, his blue beard fluttering. 'I think that Principal Krill's researches are less dependable than you believe.'

Brannart Morphail was considered both learned

and wise, and he was indeed what passed for those things at the End of Time. This put him in conflict with Principal Krill on questions of knowledge just as Volospion found himself in conflict with Lord Jagged on those of style.

'Those unsteady, changeable books you refer to are simply defective,' Krill countered now, surging forward so that he clinked against the side of his massive jar. His face flattened against the glass like a breast.

'Is the Duke here?' Morphail asked. 'You've claimed this is part of his drama.'

'Yes, but his role is to remain dead and faintly radiating in his pyramid. Have you seen the giant face on it now, and the jungle?'

'You believe the Duke of Queens – of all people – has introduced novelty.'

'He has organised for us a very fruitful confusion,' Jagged stated. 'If handled correctly, this adventure could give rise to a bonanza of new fashions and diversions. This "revolution" business for example – well, it seems a bit dry and meaningless at the moment, but it seems to have moved many people in the past. It's dynamite!'

'Dine a what?'

'Dynamite, Brannart,' said Bishop Castle. 'Krill says revolutionists used it for food. It was a powder – they just added water. And revolution can be food for our imaginations! Why, look at this thing I just thought of.' And he produced a sort of wooden trumpet, putting it to his lips and blowing a deafening blast which flumed orange slime from the bell in a storm of horror.

'This is your doing, Krill!' Morphail snapped, wiping detritus from his front. 'You and your meatball history will kill us all.'

A skeletal visage hove up at his shoulder.

'Brannart – you still have a bone companion?'

'It is I,' said Werther de Goethe mournfully, his skull-like face barely mobile. He stepped forward in a cloak of black albatross cloth. Behind him his funeral barge stood on the air jetty like a parasite.

'Oh connoisseur of chasms,' waxed Jagged, 'oh collector of cankers … a man doomed by the shadow darkening his door – and that shadow is his own!'

'You can surely help us, Werther,' said the Iron Orchid. 'None of us seem to have a firm idea of the rubric of social despair and …' – she twirled her silver-painted fingers in the air – 'repression!'

'Nonsense,' stated Werther in a voice like hollow brass. 'Our species has been arranging such horrors since we were mere abominations cooling on a beach. Few realise vacuum is an organism – one attenuated and thin-spread, but an organism for all that. And this barren entity prospers.'

'No, my dear Werther, I don't see it. People don't like such stuff.'

'Not at the mind's surface. But in its depths is the urge toward nothingness.' His eyes were tragic. 'Thus we act in the service of oblivion.'

'Groan-encumbered, unhappy Werther – where do you get such notions?'

'From grim reality,' mourned Werther, then brightened to precision. 'And the specific terminology is from Quoi Vico at the clock sanctuary. He has insight into the motivations a man hides from himself.'

'Quoi Vico?' Volospion asked with acute interest. 'Really?'

'Well!' the Orchid exclaimed suddenly, staring into mid-air. 'I have an alarm at my menagerie! Several of my creatures have been released!'

'It begins,' said Jagged, throwing a glance at the drifting Krill.

'What do you mean?' the Orchid asked.

'That the Duke's "revolutionary" has moved against our ... What was it, Krill? Empire?'

'Arrangement,' Krill pronounced without enthusiasm. 'Given our current lack of order, "empire" is somewhat of a stretch.'

'Exactly,' Bishop Castle agreed. 'Our reign of terror's barely off the ground.'

'How is it that a group of people can be more stupid than any one individual within it, or weaker, or more cruel?' The Iron Orchid smiled at the idea's visitation. 'I've often wondered.'

'Perhaps that's one of the things we'll discover,' Volospion said.

'This incident at the Orchid's menagerie,' Krill bubbled, 'points up the function of an army – of force and coercion.'

'That fat butterfly in your skull is fluttering very like a brain, Krill,' said Brannart Morphail, 'but an army? Who knows anything about it?'

'Lord Shark, perhaps?' Jagged suggested. 'Didn't he make some toy soldiers that all moved at the same time?'

'Yes,' Volospion agreed. 'He set them going and

watched them march away until they were gone. I doubt he'd be interested in all this, but we could ask. Has anyone seen him lately?'

'Not for several years,' said Bishop Castle, adjusting his gigantic hat. 'He was building some houses out of concrete blocks, when I last saw him, and measuring them.'

'He's made a study of battle strategy, I remember,' Jagged told them. 'It's terror arrayed like breakfast on a tray, leaving the battlefield in a shocking state. But we run far ahead of ourselves. We need at this time to establish our political position. And that means armoured trousers.'

'A bold project.'

'It is.'

'It could almost pass for a plan.'

'Anyway,' Jagged began.

7

RECLINING FEMALE

*In Which the Narrative of Our Knight's
Mishap is Continued*

Leo was still feeling the electric low of just indignation as he approached the two-tone dazzle-patterned towers of Regina's home. He walked across a black lawn dotted with white flowers, between grey trees like twigs which had gathered fluff, past a sundial of milk glass on to a terrace of checkered flagstones. Entering, he found that Regina's abode and everything in it was silverine and flickering, the air aswim with strange motive particles. It had been decorated piece by piece with white dove leather and hangings of midnight velvet and odd monochromed Persian rugs. On ebony floor stood a chalk piano and a smaller pearlite harpsichord. On the latter was a bowl of nuts. 'You're pretty well fixed,' he said as she followed him in. 'I thought you were a slave, Gina Sparks. And maybe you still are, in your mind. Economic slavery is a blade so sharp it takes years to realise you've been cut. Know fully that you own yourself.'

Regina sat in a giant silverlined halfshell and looked at Leo, trying to gauge his tone and intent. 'I do, Leo.'

'Enslaved by degrees nearly imperceptible to a

busy man,' Leo went on, unable to stand still. He avoided her eye like a man afraid to look into the sun. 'But only honest money retains the flavour of how it was made. Not fortune accrued irrespective of work or effort but according to luck and geography. To be dismissive of suffering one need only filter the facts obtusely: one man has a thousand dollars and another has nothing. Statistically they both have an average of five hundred dollars. The poor man in the case worked hard, the rich man in the case did nothing. On average they worked adequately for their pay. It's child's play, this sort of thing.'

'When you speak so, you are very poor company.'

'Much of people's mental energy goes into positioning themselves so that they can be surprised by results disastrous to others. It's a central component of the opt-out from consequence, a wide-eyed alibi.'

'It is said,' Regina began, pausing to summon either her memory or her imagination (assuming there was a difference in this place), 'that every act casts a shadow.'

'Correct – and most are as ineffectual. Only when enacted from a position of real power is it necessary to consider an act's far impact. Yet the common people are expected to be the conscience of their government.'

'Are these declarations preliminaries to the revolution you mentioned?'

Leo stopped, frowning at her. 'Yes. Yes, as a matter of fact they are.'

'Continue.' She rested her arms on the flanges of

the clamshell and spread her legs in comfort.

'You can spark a fire by banging two facts together. Regrettably it takes only one lie. The cloth of law is stitched with superstition and fear. And it's designed to become habitual. The vision of the future must be a sort of imperialist oblivion, lockstep and unchanging – oh, but for never-ending "improvement" of course.'

'Of course.'

'Man, bound in a common terror of honesty, marches on. But a sunflower remains a sunflower beneath the heel. "Rage at once, and absolutely"? – no, better to rage with a plan.'

He ate a nut. There wasn't any flavour – just a bit of commotion.

'What shall I do with you?' Regina said at last.

He didn't know how to answer – he hadn't had time to work out the local absolutes. She was an intensity of glowing white skin and turbo ink.

'I hope you haven't decided,' she said, 'that I'll be in the way.'

'No,' he said.

'When we want something, it's ours, Leo del Toro. For us, reality is docile. My uncle tells me that the universe – topsoil and all – is going to rack and ruin quite soon. We have only a few thousand years. The stars are going out – it is the End of Time. But using technology found amid the old cities we can focus all the remaining cosmic power to fulfil whatever desires we have. We have re-fertilised the sun. And this – all this – is like a place we dream of and then awake to find we are alive within.'

'These are the ideas of a crazy person.'

'We stimulate bursts of life, as when you blow on a cooling coal,' she continued. 'We cultivate distinctions productive of humour, and of effect, and ornament. It speeds up the endtime a little, but otherwise it's harmless.'

'Stop saying all this.' He had no use for her doting lunacy. It was embarrassing to him.

'You may have to swallow your opinions like thorns. They are probably true, in whatever strange circumstance you are used to, but they do not apply here. Dust be diamonds, water be wine.'

'Pack it in will you?'

A foreign moment as he looked beyond her at a small sight buried in the window, a lozenge of sky, shallow clouds like the worn faces on coins. When he looked back to her she bent her head like the tipping of a wing.

Leo felt his heart blush. 'Uh,' he said.

'What?'

'Nothing,' he whispered, staring at her. He was suspended. He had reckoned without the transparent counterweight of the emotions.

He had to get organised.

'You say this world is old,' he said quietly. 'An old mind may grow complex or simple. The latter is the laziness of empire at last, when a hierarchy of puppets will tangle together.'

'Speak to them about it. They've spun up what they're calling an "imperial palace" next to Lord Jagged's home. They're waiting for you, very interested.'

'How do you know.'

'They're telling me.'

'Telling you. Now?'

'Yes.'

'In your head, I suppose?'

'Yes.'

He sat at last, on the piano stool, and felt strangely dishevelled. 'If any of this is true, and if you can replicate objects. You can help me.'

He thought about it.

'*Will* you help me?'

'Of course I will.'

'Bloodthirsty but weary – that's the kind of enemy I favour,' he said, but found himself thinking *Women only like me for my mind.*

8

THE GRAND INQUISITOR

*A Childish Incident In Which, However, Our Knight is
Seen Pursing His Lips to Deadly Effect*

The dome was tattooed with insect feathers in the
fragile style of lithographed tin. At the landing bay
door, Volospion was staring into the climate. He
called back at the others. 'Regina says he's on his
way.'

'Quickly,' panicked Bishop Castle, 'shall we create
some people for him to organise?' Today his head was
perched atop a carving like stacked plate mushrooms.
A radiance of crystalline hair surrounded this head,
a mineral mane that broke and powdered as he was
bustled toward the throne.

'Too late, dear friend,' said Lord Jagged. 'Time to
act high and mighty, pronto. An expression of outrage
is timetabled for 3pm. To your places!'

Fifty or more 'courtiers' arrayed themselves at
the walls, including several golden turtles wearing
saffron scarves. Among them was a dragon like a wet
decoration. There was a very tall, thin man in a green
and black striped garter-snake suit, who had a head
roughly the size of an acorn. Another had the body
of a man and the legs of a policeman. All held opera
glasses and were very excited.

'It was you, Bishop, who insisted on playing the Emperor first. Now recall the archive materials and distil it down to a passable despot. It need only be accurate enough to signify the role to the other players in our little drama.'

'How shall I conceal my true feelings?'

'Hide them in your cheeks. Or better still, your knees – it's the last place he'll think to look.'

'I fear we haven't the ancient nuances ...'

'Here is the method I recommend,' stated Jagged, sitting Bishop Castle down. 'Doctor your powers so that you are more frustrated, and so will hunger for influence, you see? I cannot predict the full spectrum of symptoms that may result. Discipline with dozens of miseries an hour causing bizarre lack and worry ...'

'For me?'

'For your subjects.'

'My "subjects",' repeated Castle, his spiral ears of neon flashing on and off in alarm.

'And at any moment you might be asked something. Begin your response with "I have made it clear that..."'

'Then what?'

'Anything you like. The important message is the "made it clear", especially claiming it's already been done and that you're merely reaffirming it now.'

'I don't understand. Is it a game?'

'In a way. I mean, it's largely ceremonial. None of the people here are the people affected. And what else do we say – remember?'

'One should look at each case on its own merits,'

Bishop Castle recited. 'And we can't comment on individual cases.'

'Perfect. And don't be surprised if he bites your nose.'

'I hope he does. It will ...' Castle seemed uncertain and wary. 'Teach me a lesson?'

'Precisely.'

Castle smiled, pleased and relieved.

'Now get rid of these concrete vestments and spin up a tyrant. Volospion and I will be at your ear.'

'Is the scene viable?' asked the Iron Orchid.

'I believe it is,' said Lord Jagged, becoming a furless raccoon with eyes like bubbles. 'As far as it needs to be.'

'It's a good piece of work,' Volospion added tersely, shrinking into the form of a spider. Then everyone turned to watch the gourd-like air-barge of Profumo the Monkey cant over the landing stage, its unnecessary vortical underjets snorting flumes of noxious gas and burnt air in at the assembly. It dropped hog-like trotters, descended in swirls of dirt and slammed to the platform, its ancient engine grinding to a stop.

'Profumo,' stated the Iron Orchid. 'Why does he do it, I wonder?'

'He has made an interesting choice,' Jagged chittered from the floor. 'To be smelly, and inconvenient.'

'I suppose he helps us to appreciate those things which are not unwelcome,' the Orchid conceded with diffidence as she became a large ornamental flower which was tilted to view Profumo's emergence from the air-barge. Profumo was a homunculus with an overgrown bald head, his mouth always smiling and his forehead always frowning, his slitted eyes always watering. He looked thus now toward the entrance an instant before Leo del Toro kicked him in the pants, pitching him over the platform edge into empty air.

The courtiers were still applauding as del Toro strode into the audience hall. His new purple leather coat and gloves clashed richly with the rose quartz amphitheatre and its windows of stained Venice glass. He glanced at the courtiers, the long hanging flags and banners bearing talismanic admissions of fear, and at the gigantic veiny head which hovered in pride of place, glowing green and looking indignant at nothing in particular.

'Young man!' bellowed the head. 'What do you see?'

'A face that raises more questions than it answers, with a pulverised nose.'

'Your argument does not admit of the slightest refutation, nor cause the slightest concern to those in power. I am the Great and Powerful Odds, true and oak-solid sovereign. And you enter my empire, blaming everything that moves, killing governors hand-over-fist and releasing slaves like there was no tomorrow.'

'Well from what I've heard -'

'Silence! You are headstrong and rambunctious – a busy man. You brandished a blade, your motivations opaque, boring, and instantly confirmed. I do not embellish or understate when I tell you your malice, hectoring and baneful influence have caught our attention on two occasions. And your antics have done little to relieve the tensions upon which our empire is contingent.'

'One more mark against you,' said del Toro. 'Your case has become catastrophic.'

'Am I to be spared nothing!' roared the head. 'From a mere adventurer who sloganeers as others breathe.'

'Is that correct? Or even amusing?'

The head was silent a while, merely broiling in the air. Then it said: 'You underestimate me if you cannot see beyond this olive-green jowly head.'

'I can,' said Leo, approaching and walking through the green face. It faded and disappeared behind him as he stopped before the solid form of the Emperor sprawled in a throne of red meat.

Decked out in his state robes of pink and black check, Odds bore polished armoured trousers and the head of a cocker spaniel, albeit with a wooden beard inset with diamonds. He was septic with medals. His hands were malice hooks of bleeding metal. This composite monster was drinking cobalt milk, his canine jaws crunching clouded jewels. And he was wearing a cape. Pensive, he seemed to notice Leo for the first time. 'Well! I wonder you can look me in the face!'

'Now don't be silly.' Del Toro produced a polished chrome device and pointed it at Odds. 'I didn't hesitate in hijacking that orangutan's ship, so you can see I'm not to be trifled with.'

'Hijacked? I'm not familiar with the term.'

Del Toro seemed momentarily fazed, then

explained clearly: 'I forced the driver to help me steal the vehicle.'

'Ah!' A sigh of enlightenment echoed through the courtiers' galleries. Del Toro was peering at the Emperor's pets. A spider with an abdomen like a melon hung from a thread of piano wire, fiddling its legs like clockwork; and a trembling, jittery chipmunk stared bug-eyed from aside the throne. 'This kingdom of yours,' said del Toro, 'is like something you won at a fairground. I think I could help you put an end to what is clearly a humiliating fiasco.'

'Is that your estimation? Really?'

'It's superficial in all but its inequalities, with an inclination to falsehood and the menacing potency of arbitrary law, enlisting its own citizens to patch and maintain the illusion of their freedom. Claiming more for it does it a disservice.'

Bishop Castle, frowning out through the gluey eyes of Linden Odds, was baffled.

'Question his reasoning,' whispered Jagged.

'How do you, an interloper without responsibilities, reach such a judgement?'

'I confess I began with the assumption that it resembles other administrations. And I do admit things seem a bit off.' Del Toro was looking at the severin windows and statues of naked flames. His face became unfocussed with doubt, his voice vague. 'It all seems to have been created with a ... a sort of shallow recklessness. It's as if you're coming at it new like angels ... learning math and moths the same.' Then he seemed to recall himself, becoming rigid again with dignity. 'But all this serves for stronger crystallization.'

Castle leant to the spider. 'Angels?'

'Small overhead accusers,' Volospion provided in a whisper. He was a connoisseur of holy oddments.

Castle returned his attention to del Toro. 'Well. Where to begin?'

'A troy ounce of honesty would kill you. But you wouldn't drink. I'll stop at nothing. A fairly modest onslaught will probably suffice.'

'It sounds expedient.'

'It is, if done properly.'

'A generous response. A single blade for us all. But this outright have-an-apple revolution you crave – what's in it for us, for me? It would seem to rather put me in a cramped, minor role.'

'There's nothing in it for you but release. Mastery, after all, may be proof against wonder.'

'Yes, you seem to be complaining merely that what we do with our power lacks imagination. Happy people don't think of such things. The problem lies with you. Leo del Toro must work upon himself, and change himself into a happy man. This rebelliousness – maybe the mood will pass. It's merely a piece of mischief that has not turned out well for you, eh?'

Castle's suggestion was heard with frigid severity by the young visitor.

'Well,' Castle resumed, 'your wonderful costume has given everyone something to think about. And I have been sufficiently informed to consult with my advisors on the matter. Excuse me just a moment.'

Bishop Castle huddled with Jagged, Volospion and the Iron Orchid.

'An authentic viewpoint,' hissed Volospion, 'a ... a

stand! Yes, that's it – and he won't be shilly-shallied!'

'And what is that?' asked Castle.

'Shilly-shallying,' Jagged provided. 'The wrinkling of a man's skin by being tugged this way and that for a long time. Finally the skin would have to be shrugged off and abandoned as impractical.'

'Like a serpent?'

'Precisely. I have here an ancient photograph of a man who allowed himself to be shilly-shallied – Sam Beckett, a private detective. You see? And because he perversely refused to shed that skin – bearing it as evidence of how much he had been shilly-shallied in the course of his investigations – he was killed over a period of four nights.'

'Four nights?'

'In a church. He was being shilly-shallied even at the end, you see. The Dawn Ages were particularly cruel.'

'What about del Toro's injunction to collapse? Should we start doing it now?'

'Empires don't just collapse by themselves,' said Jagged. 'They need to be attacked.'

'I daresay it's more of a mix?' the Orchid suggested from the metal funnel of her bloom. 'They need a final push, certainly.'

'Well then, haven't we had it,' stressed Castle, 'what with having endured that violent tongue-lashing? It's disaster for us.'

'*Why* is it?' Volospion demanded.

'Doctor Volospion is correct,' Jagged stated. 'Toro has no authority and so his words are nothing to us. It is not for us to decide we are done for and begin to organise our fall. The onus is on del Toro to topple us against our will, you see?'

'I suppose,' Castle muttered.

The chipmunk seemed to be showing Odds a photograph of the playwright Samuel Beckett. Odds himself didn't have the face of a despot. It was too dramatic, like a movie villain. This was someone's idea of what a tyrant should look like, not the mundane or even comical appearance of the real thing.

Leo had noticed that his words were being met not with scorn or outrage but a sort of entranced attention, and a shallow one. They looked back at him with eyes like toothpaste. He had the sickly sensation that everything around him, people and all, were a kind of plastic fungal excrescence, false throughout and sweating toxins. No oxygen entered or exited. It was unbreathing nightmare. And it tasted familiar.

But flattered, perhaps, by the influx of outcomes which he could interpret as being dependent on himself, he had allowed himself to be delayed several minutes. *The truth can be as hot and transparent as aniseed*, he thought.

Odds turned from the huddle with his pets and addressed Leo. 'Now, young man. D'you know, when I heard about a benign eccentric hulking about and disagreeing I asked my advisers, "What's the meaning of this?" – and they replied, "Three words, your Majesty: Leo del Toro. A corruptive influence, and energetic." They described your snorting bicycle and preposterous shirt. And so the people have asked that I deal with this dangerous radish.'

The chipmunk chittered frantically at him from the foot of the throne.

'Radical, even,' Odds clarified. 'Ah yes, you're the rebel for me. But on principle I can't negotiate with such people – at least, not until I do. In any case, I wish you the very best.'

The chipmunk screamed up at Odds.

'I mean,' Odds continued abruptly, 'I couldn't help thinking that if I released you, you'd be sprouting a real top-notch one of these revolutions you seem partial to. Pretty soon I'd have dozens of revolutionaries crowding in here, pushing and shoving for advantage. What is this thing anyway – a snail?'

Odds reached for the gun and Leo backed up fast. 'Don't move!' He fired at the spider, which splashed apart in a green blur. This received a cheer from the courtiers.

'But we have discussed in detail your sad mania,' Odds continued, sitting back again complacently. 'The only way you know you've spoken is that people look away. At such a level of powerlessness, cause and effect is rendered void – there is no personal experience or evidence of that principle. So how can such an ineffectual being ever be convinced he can change a world? As far as he's concerned, he has no definite connection with it. But I suppose pre-embittered visitors save time, eh Jagged? I mean, er ... Myrtle. Anyway, we speak of grey being almost black, but not of black being almost grey. Thus the status quo has inherent strength. One step beyond order lies chaos. I suggest you go down on every free knee and beg to join us.'

Leo gave an indifferent grunt. 'The idea's sole claim to my mind lies in the example of others – these others seem dull beyond measure, and unduly limited. No, clearly it's not for me. You're glib with power.'

'Thus I give my account with an effortless brevity which the people's dull faculties, cowardice and stupid assumptions will work to enrich and amplify.'

'Ah, so *your* lies are *special*. Well, I find your rather proprietary way with reality demeaning. And I see no particular advantage in postponing your downfall.'

The end was surprising, like pure discovery. Leo reached a gloved hand to flap open his coat, exposing the explosive vest.

'He's wearing a *girdle!*' gasped the Emperor an instant before undergoing an explosion big enough to blow the eyebrows off the face of god.

9

TODAY AND TOMORROW:
THE AGE OF FRUSTRATION

What Happened to Leo del Toro Upon His Resurrection

In his chest, a heartful of bloody teeth. But he was sure he'd been borne to the skies by a blast of noble fire. Certainly he was dead. 'My destiny is over, maybe,' he considered. 'And now, at last: some lethargy.'

Breath asserted itself. He awoke in a bolt of bewilderment.

'Hold – he rouses!'

It was night. A wet jungle of tattooed leaves. A cobra with six opalescent wings played a Cuban organ orientale, lit by the alternations of a complicated stoplight. A bullfrog as big as a bulldozer, its skin glistening like ocean-sprayed rock, stared. It was joined by a self-satisfied-looking gargoyle whose midsection was a turning carousel upon which small versions of himself rode smiling and waving. There was a sort of blue octopus in a huge jar on wheels. Smeared torchflames, blotted faces, blank expectancy and opaque stares.

Leo was a headache with snowballs for eyes, a membrane away from hell. The full realisation of survival made him grimace.

'We welcome you, Master del Toro. You have been

missing too long from the feast.'

'Welcome?'

Leo had awoken into a celebration of sorcerers. At its core were Lord Jagged, Doctor Volospion, the Iron Orchid, Principal Krill and Bishop Castle. Around them were Baron Coma, Mistress Christia the Everlasting Concubine, Jack-in-the-Green, O'Kala Incarnadine, Whisper Terrible, Corporal Pork of the Spammer Gain, Profumo the Monkey, Jherek Carnelian, Falcomatis of the Jet Black Trauma Feathers, Sweet Orb Mace, Again the Shuttle Clue, Brannart Morphail, Roxanne Ansari, Ulysses the Overwhale, the Earl of Carbolic, the Luton Clown, Gaf the Horse in Tears, Argonheart Po, Pastor Bulbous and the piratical Fox Grave. Around the fringes were sundry creatures, some owlish and others like mustachioed prawns.

The celebrants were gathered at the base of the golden pyramid about which the sweating jungle had recently grown. It was a clearing lit by pan sconces floating in mid-air and hung with leopard balloons and zebra bunting. Vivid grandees ate perfumed dates and little cupcakes coloured green and silver. The front slope of the pyramid bore the Duke's profile like a titanic triangular coin.

Doctor Volospion helped Leo to his feet (an innovative overture instantly envied by the rest) and swiped crinkled blue leaves from the rebel's coat. Volospion was wearing a cloak of zild velvet, and Leo, having never seen this particular colour before, at first perceived a broiling gap where the cloak should have been. Gradually this flurrying absence resolved into a startling visceral flavour that made Leo feel slightly larger and smokier than he was.

'Confused by your own persistence?' the Doctor asked. 'Regina resurrected Jagged here and the Iron Orchid, and the three of them set to spinning the rest of us up again. That accomplished, we resurrected you.'

'Our civilisation is a phoenix tree,' Lord Jagged explained smoothly, 'able to re-grow from the smallest fragment. So long as one of us remains who recalls how it was, it can be recreated. Not unsettled by resurrection are you?' His tone was disingenuous.

'Drink on, strange world!' called Bishop Castle, raising and quaffing a cup of limonata.

'That explosion, Toro,' cried the Iron Orchid. 'Such a surprise! A masterstroke!'

'A consummate inferno,' Jagged agreed.

'Indeed your bursting me with that hand-held device was rather startling too,' Volospion added rather diffidently. 'Though I wish you'd offered me some warning so that I could have braced myself to fully savour the experience.'

The Iron Orchid seemed exasperated. 'Volospion, when will you learn to allow life to, as it were, wash over you? Do you believe for instance that in antique times people asked eachother to brace themselves for such assaults?'

'I believe the Sundance Kid was heard to say "Tense your hips centrally" before dropping a boulder on the owner of a tin mine,' said Volospion with dignity.

'I suppose My Lady Charlotina told you that little tale. She will say anything to encourage more inventive lovemaking.'

'Worry not,' Jagged confided to Leo. 'The imperial palace was quickly restored to its previous condition.'

'I'm lost,' Leo muttered.

'You're a triumph, del Toro,' hailed Bishop Castle, pointing at him with his ecclesiastical gearstick. 'Your decorous mayhems have us covered in a honey glaze of ... well what, my buffed and polished Orchid?'

'Honey?'

'The honey of dissent!'

'The pollen of disgruntlement!'

'Here's to plain speaking! In any case we haven't had a visitor of your calibre for years, I suppose. All wish to be seen with you. And Krill – this huge lubberfiend over here – wants to sing you a song.'

Several of the vat squid's treacly eyes started open and it began to protest its outraged disinclination from a mouth slack as a sack.

Looking at the white vine spiralled around a tree's vertical ribs, Leo thought of Regina. And at that moment she arrived in a black diamond carriage drawn by six white old-man kangaroos.

'A carriage like a treasure chest on wheels,' marvelled Bishop Castle, helping her down. 'And six white boomers! You halftone minx, you've done it again!'

'Thank you, Bishop. Is the guest of honour revived yet?'

Bishop Castle called to Volospion. 'Doctor, will you rouse the Duke? No need to start anew, his body's in this pyramid thing – just get him up and puffing, eh?'

'I already have, Bishop,' said Volospion. 'And here he is, I think.'

All turned to the edifice of artificially-aged gold. The long stone ramp, its steps clotted with rusty leaves, bore the gilded form of the Duke of Queens. This figure of flowing robes and gold scrollwork descended with a look of amiable bewilderment, his spread arms a concession to theatricality.

Bishop Castle stepped forward, his vestments snagging on the pink blades of Corporal Pork's antlers. He tore it free and turned back to the Duke. 'My dear Duke – how "the hell" are you?'

'I am returned from the steamy afterworld. Was the party a success?'

'Success, he says! You're the talk of society, Duke. Prolific calendar windows pitch asunder for your attendance.'

'Really?' the Duke asked, his face open and surprised.

'All cues were taken. We have been busily disporting ourselves as kings and presidents.'

'I have felt oddly elevated by this bitter enhancement of thought,' claimed the Iron Orchid. 'It feels rather like illness. A sort of cold fever which sends the mind sideways.'

'Our own Bishop Castle here set out to mimic one mad with power and was entirely equal to the task,' Volospion explained.

'We've done a lot of growing up lately, we can tell you,' giggled Castle. 'The new seriousness! The new vogue!'

'Uncle!' Regina cried, flying into his arms. 'Dear Duke! The party was wonderful! And its aftermath has fascinated everyone!'

'In - indeed?'

'All have worked to support you, Duke,' said the Iron Orchid. 'I know you'll be pleased. And we have enjoyed the antics of your charismatic maverick, Leo del Toro.'

'Who?'

'This fantastic adventurer over here. The fellow is a culminator – stirs everything to the boil. Where did you find him? Or did you spin him up yourself?'

There was silence as the Duke approached Leo del Toro, and scrutinised the dented helm of his face in the flickering torchlight.

'This? I do not know the man!'

'Ha!' Volospion clapped his hands like a pistol shot.

'I seem to recall him jabbing me with some tin ...'

'There! You see, Jagged?' Volospion crowed. 'The boy's feral! An accident here, probably a time traveller! And the Duke's success likewise an accident and a failure!'

'Really, Doctor, have a care,' Lord Jagged of Canaria responded mildly. 'An accident, a feral interloper, and you deem it a failure? I consider this of greater value than if del Toro were a mere artifact cast by the Duke.'

'Perhaps. Yet simultaneously you absent yourself from the significance of these events.'

'Wandering perfectly satisfied, that is my nature,' Jagged stated blandly.

Volospion eyed him with suspicion, tempted to erupt with sarcasm. But recalling his advantage, he grinned sharply. 'The fact remains – I win the wager.'

STEVE AYLETT

Jagged ignored him, taking the Duke of Queens by both hands. 'Talented Duke,' he pronounced. 'Congratulations. It is the event of the season. Let us celebrate this success!'

A cheer went up, and a massive centipede with segments like leather armchair cushions started dancing, followed by other guests who lay on the floor and started moving like snakes, sending S-shaped waves along their bodies for no reason. Many surged forward to lavish fond admiration on their rejuvenated friend and Bishop Castle was toppled at last with the weight of his head-dress. Bent on mutual tolerance, albino ravens and heart-shaped robins bowed at one another in the trees.

Leo grabbed Regina by the arm and hauled her aside, hissing at her. 'Reconstruction of what was destroyed? What could possess you to do something so foolish? We're back where we started!'

'Werther de Goethe informed me this was the precise meaning of "revolution". Try some food. Argonheart Po has created a maze of lime jelly which you can eat your way through in a straight line.'

'I was at the other party, remember. Those so-called sausages tasted like mud and the jam didn't taste of anything. I have been *damned!* At a stroke I see the exposed clockwork of your morality. Look at that so-called Duke of yours.'

The dazed Duke was lost amid a storm of boisterous jitterbug dancing.

'Fabulating and spectating: that's his life.'

'He has sought knowledge,' Regina observed, 'and then built beauty into any gaps. Would that everyone was so harmless, and so dear.'

He looked at the big loving cartoon bombs of her eyes, the crazy particles in her skin. 'I suppose,' he said lamely, breaking off. He gazed up at twinkling darkness. 'I can't tell what are stars and what are leaves.'

'The stars are dying, the leaves neither live nor die. We made them.'

'Everything's dying and you suck the remaining vitality all the harder.'

'Yes.'

'Hastening the end. Oh, Gina, get me out of here. Please, let's go.'

Regina touched a power ring on her left hand and she and Leo disappeared – reversing light ate the air where they had sat.

'It's daylight here, high summer I think.'

They sat on an ottoman in a tile court surrounded by date palms and she oaks. The courtyard was decorated with giant decorative urns, a blushed fluorite bust of someone whose name Regina had forgotten, and a pulsing fountain. Some perfectly round rubies lay scattered here and there. A large green moon and a small grey moon hung near the sun. At the End of Time, full-scale planetary bodies were almost everybody's cup of tea – sometimes for habitation but more usually for the wonderful ambience they cast.

Leo's head was bowed, his hair like black vinyl. She did not know how to begin with him.

'Show me again,' he said. 'Your magic.'

Pleased, she touched a power ring. A butterfly with stained glass wings folded out of it and fluttered toward the cobalt sky, landing upon it. The sky cracked like a mirror and remade itself before it could fall. Her new sky was strawberry static, fizzing like soda. In all it was difficult to conceive of a sky so thoroughly taken by surprise. 'See? The world is everlasting – it's coming and it's going.'

But Leo seemed disturbed by something in the wasteland of pink mud beyond the trees. 'What is that?'

It looked like the archway of a church warped back into the metal ribcage of an enormous dinosaur.

'Scene creep,' she told him. 'The edge of a creation extending of its own momentum and making strange shapes. They call this landscape Conception Junction.' She gazed at the trampled landscape with the imprint of various departed dreams across it. None of it matched. 'When two projects mix up at the edges it makes them harder for their creators to disassemble – it leaves a knot, a clot, you see?'

'Useless, like old bubblegum.'

'And losing its flavour, that's right. That bit looks like a sort of church dome made of orange scaffolding all melted down, doesn't it?'

Leo seemed baffled, bothered. She was both astonished and confused by him: he was sometimes the magnificent stranger with about him a fierce industry of self. At other times he was an over-heated poet in his highest power, bringing his febrile anger into art. And at other times a lifeless, stunned, lost soul. At such moments he seemed to piece himself together again with words. He gathered himself now. 'Your people, these fantastics tantamount to gods, and their dilute sacrament, an incontinent magic – it operates at a level of consumption incompatible with nature. This "magic" of yours doesn't even have any workings.'

'The workings are in the old cities, Leo, as I told you. Ancient machines underground focus the energy of surrounding space and put it at our service. The rings only focus that energy, according to our will.'

'Words, like dreams, are informed by our lives, so don't assume my words mean the same as yours. By "workings" I mean ritual, the use of … some sort of knowledge. Not just wishing on a star.'

'The Duke says we have paradise without forfeiture.'

'You don't *know* what you've forfeited. You've forgotten, or it was forfeited before your birth. This random time is varnished thinly with politeness and without enough nourishment even for the grave. A blissless passivity. That you accede to this, Regina … I wish I didn't feel disappointed in you. I don't have the right, after all.'

'It isn't blissless. We can create freely. We can have whatever we want. Where you're from, it's not like this?'

'No. But everyone acts as if it was. It's called "denial".'

'That's the name of where you're from?'

Leo stared at her, then seemed to give something up. 'Yes.'

'We infer entire landscapes from your language.

Having heard of your musical blue grass, we recreate that, and complement it logically with a singing green sky. You could tell my friends about your time – they're very interested, and so am I.'

'Really?'

'Yes. For instance, were mountains bigger than cities? Did people wear more than one shirt? Did people have more than one idea? That sort of thing.'

'In my time each privation endured at least a thousand years, the progress of society was the forging of replacement shackles, and I dedicated my life to those who were so enslaved. This I've pursued for love's sake. And it seems I'm to be humoured – laughed at fondly like an old man's anger.'

She laughed. 'You resemble Li Pao in his sulks and occasional angers. He too is ... serious-minded, in a way. Though he has become much used to our ways, I think. He seems sometimes to need reminding of his objections.' He did not join her mirth, and she became silent. Then she asked, more quietly, 'Why must you think of these things?'

Leo seemed sad. He looked down at the patio dotted with titian rubies. 'It comes to me like the talons of two ideas carving against each other, insupportable. They tear at my mind, and I have to end the pain.' He pushed at some jewels with his boot. 'Some injustices are an agony even to contemplate.'

'Then why contemplate them?'

'That's the choice, of course. Change yourself into something that doesn't care, or be the person you are, and care, and try to ease the pain by attacking the injustice. And then there are always more.'

'Not always. We have heard from many scientists and travellers that time is drawing to a close. We have only a few thousand years or so. Surely this is a comfort?'

'That the universe will end without knowing justice? No, somehow that doesn't quite do it for me.' After a while he looked at her. 'I'm sorry, Gina, you're right that I'm not very good company. Rude, even. And I doubt I'm very entertaining for you or your friends.' He seemed honestly unhappy. 'It sounds an exaggeration, but a sense of justice is a wound open to every infection the world can cook up. You end as a sort of towering toxicity, and as much a procession of one as you started. And still in the right, probably. Even the most outrageously painful feelings become familiar, with the knowledge that they're survivable. It's like realising – or remembering – you can survive in the vacuum of space, or underwater, or in acid.'

'Human beings aren't meant to survive in those conditions, are they?'

'No. But I mean that the most terrible pain is survivable. It's almost surprising.'

'Yours seems to have been a society of strange ... endurances. Perhaps ... perhaps you don't understand us! You're wrong to think our world is random or our behaviour chaotic. Here, all is creatable. Therefore there are decisions to be made in every direction.'

'You stand on the shoulders of giants and ... juggle with starfruit.'

She understood approximately what he was on about. 'Well, some of our world is still original: the dead cities, for instance. We allow some attractive natural distress patterns to remain uncorrected. Have you noticed that the moon, the real one I think, has grown branches of dust, dirty trails hanging behind it? It's interesting. Brannart Morphail says it's part of the universal collapse.'

Leo scowled and muttered, 'Of course. Apocalypse is pretty.'

She could no longer ignore his apparent malice. 'Why are you so harsh? Why do you talk this way? Don't you like me?'

He looked heartbroken. 'I love you, Gina. You're amazing. That's why I wish I thought higher of you. Do you love? How can you love with irony, with a capricious decision? It's not love at all.'

'You said you acted from love of your shackled people, with a decision and a plan.'

He seemed weary now, barely anguished. 'As a demonstration. That love wasn't a whim of fashion and nor were my actions. But this pocket hell of yours is all spectacle. Nothing is raw and unfinished, and yet nothing is really ripe, either. It's a scentless flower, Regina.'

'It is not my world.'

'Why do you say that?'

She frowned. 'I don't ... I don't know.'

'Perhaps you become ashamed of it as you should.' He stood up. 'No, that's nonsense. I'm sorry. If this is where things were headed all the time, I accept it. The world ends not with a bang nor a whimper, but with clowns. Empty and painted. So it is. Now's the time.'

He gave a stiff nod of assent to something in his own mind, and walked away. As he dwindled into the wasteland, Regina felt something she didn't understand. Why was she sad that he had stopped shouting? Why did his acceptance of her world feel like a sort of tragedy? He had been a man with a purpose, she supposed – something new, certainly. And now he was like one of those machines in the old cities that didn't have a use and weren't connected to anything. It was strange. He had not died, but was like a ghost. She would have to ask Lord Jagged about it.

Regina held up her bare arm palm-inward and watched the tattooed vines reform into a likeness of Leo, fiery hair blazing from his head. Colour began to crawl up her arm.

10

THE FOOTSTEPS DIE OUT FOR EVER

Which All Who Have No Sense,
Will Think to Contain Much Ado About Nothing

My heart has turned white, he thought. As he crossed the desert, thwarted exasperation starkened into despair. Now where was the man incapable of self-pity? The man who stitched his own wounds? Had he been reconstituted without a soul? Had it been docked like a dog's tail?

He couldn't get any traction on this new world, could not see how it oriented around his loyalties. The moment he arrived here his dignity and control had begun to evaporate. Of course – because these were qualities sustained by the knowledge of effectiveness. He had always taken the success of revolution as an inevitability, on the condition that it was worked toward without cease. Was this decorated desolation really the result? Adrift in a faithless and factless chaos, he thirsted for some rich node of continuity, like the Arabian coffee urn forever on the boil.

A history ripe with people is forgotten. Value is forgotten. Meaning is forgotten. And what's forgotten might as well never have existed. He was not sure he believed this last, but he was closer to believing it now than he had ever been.

He staggered through fickle seasons, random darkness and daylight, the ruins of incredible heavens – a polychrome clutter which formed a crust over exhausted land. He could not travel so many days of broken distance without perceiving the thinness of its recycled miracles, painted as they were around a juiceless planet. At one point he saw in the landscape a figure riding a massive white scarab beetle with pool-cue antennae and foreclaws resembling a bitten sandwich, but it was soon out of sight. At another time a swordfish air barge passed overhead. He did not pause to examine a colossal shattered visage half-sunk in the sand, resembling as it did Stan Laurel. A pharmaceutical-grade sunset brought with it a thin silent convoy of aircars which seemed to be travelling a parallel frequency, stretching and trickling sidelong across the horizon. He passed a range of glass mountains, created and abandoned, and far castles like sports trophies.

His body was stiff and he breathed like stone. Veins pumped unimportance to and from his heart. The fear he had seen in others now walked at his side. His identity had become an ordeal mask with inner blades. And the theft of his usual pain was unexpected. 'Rage, return,' he rasped through split lips. 'You must carry me through this wilderness.'

Whether it was his own inner gloom or he had entered a bleaker geographical territory (or both), he could not tell. The desert was now black salt and lava rock like coal coral. Beside a dark-misted abyss of hollow whispers and ignoble gasses stood the charred diagonals of a palatial ruin. Leo fell into his own shadow. And crawling toward the shelter of the arched landscape, he raised his eyes to meet those of a blank, doll-hard face. Flanked by a couple of scorched and ruined walls, a figure in black velvet sat in a dull throne of smoked quartz, his posture that of a smashed crane fly. Cupped in his hands was a near-dead rose of which one petal remained red and vivid. He was haloed by an atomised atmosphere, hours and minutes falling to die around him. Above him, incomplete strands of sky hung down like hair. This phantom seemed in fact like a big snake of smoke in which a skull hovered. He reminded Leo of a painting he had once seen of a man visiting Hastings Pier. What was it called? Of course – *The Scream.*

The pale, long face addressed Leo from amid whisking smithereens of torn ash. 'You are the new time traveller. The new magician. I am Werther the Unfortunate. I will not welcome you. My presence erases welcome.'

'Am I really seeing you? Where am I?'

'Failing and filthy, faded of faith, you reach Werther's sterile promontory. Perchance you project your inner world more than you think, oh weary visitor. Why else do you and I meet at this time? We mourn the catalogue of errors which led to the creation of this existence. We are alike. Perhaps because I was born, not made. Little did I think then that I should journey this road. Luck is energy. Both good and bad luck exist. And, like energy, neither can be created or destroyed. We find ourselves chosen by stings in a boundless ocean.'

Distantly, Leo knew he should feel insulted. 'You don't know me.'

'I hear your sighs. Such sighs have an impermeable surface, they are private. But what need to look inside you, or you into me, when we can see the truth all about us? Despair is honest. Its content is the same as its exterior.'

'What's that in your hand?'

Seeming to recall its presence, Werther quickly flattened the near-living rose in his hand and showed his palms. 'Nothing.' Though Leo noticed the wraith's fingers bore several pearly rings.

'As I was saying,' the shade continued, 'no hope exists – I was born into this hearse of ribs, surrounded already with these worn curses: the incomprehensible skeleton of history, tribal authority bound by a thin bit of cosmic fortune, the court of knaves, the sterility of prestige, desires common as statues rooted only by their weight, false chains grown heavy, true chains grown heavier, the day's pointless idyll and the dead hand of nature. This world is a doorknob that spins without engaging. Join sorrowful Werther in the heady glare of the constant end. I am smoking eighty cigarettes a day.'

'I'm ... sorry to hear it,' said Leo, disoriented under the doom-laden stare of this nonreflective man. He was numb, severed from his own words. 'Maybe ... I'm just tapped out, temporarily.'

'Plans and intentions net objects together. Without plans – for instance upon utter, drastic failure – reality is again perceived directly, each part in its own right. Leave your hopes behind. The weight of character, its all-elbows complication, spoils the aerodynamics of the soul.'

All but his assumptions were unassailable. 'I don't care to fly,' Leo told him.

Werther reached into the sand and pulled up a chain of hearts, trinket organs ticking out of unison. These immediately decayed and blew away as dust. 'The ancient Sumerians developed a magical system of failure. They had as many names for failure as Eskimos had for snow. If you know all the ways things fail, you have a multidimensional map that is categorically sublime. The smallest conceivable portion of time supplies us with ample tragedy for a lifetime; and each and every smallest portion of a lifetime does supply it. Consciousness is a miniature variation on the error at large. Each tear contains a hologram of its cause. The truth comes gradually, passed slowly from failure to failure. This is the only progress possible in the Errorverse and the despair delivery system some call "the world".'

Leo opened his mouth a little but could say nothing. Werther was like a wall of screed, but in his current degree-zero state Leo hadn't the wherewithal or energy to challenge him.

'I know,' sighed Werther, inconsolable. 'Repartee is the answer to ashes, being ashes itself. We are sifting meaning from dust. Death suppresses theory completely in a silence broken only by insects.'

Something landed on Leo's arm. A white moth with silver eyes like cake beads. It twitched away again, disappearing.

'Beauty isn't the final version,' Werther whispered.

'The winners write the histories,' Leo said, reciting an idea he'd got too used to to let go. 'But only if they can be bothered, I suppose. These people here ...'

Werther nodded slowly, seeming to consider and finally decide upon a disclosure. 'Doctor Volospion owns an ancient scroll on rare cerebral membrane vellum. I doubt he understands what he has, there. It tells the story of a collector of religious relics, much like Volospion himself. The old man in the story has several of Christ's anklebones, at least a dozen of his fingers, gallons of his blood, three of his skulls at various stages of development and so on. He determines to piece them together into a Tauksaw, a re-assembled body, the ultimate object of worship. In his cloistered chamber he thinks he hears the faintest "click" with each incorporation. Of course, at last the result is a monster. An incoherent mass of fraud, fakery, lies, deception, self-deception and even honest delusion. It rears up, each patch carving one against another. The old man is horrified. "What are you?" he demands. "You have achieved what I never quite achieved in life," states the abomination. "I asked," the old man repeats, "what are you?" "I am what you have made me," says the freak. "What?" asks the old man. "A liar? A pointless mess? A justification for anything?" "Yes," says the figure. "A man."'

The slow rain of feathery smuts continued to fall, grey and dull like sedation. Leo felt as if he'd been interred. And he had to know all this creature would tell him.

'What is the Errorverse?'

'It is known that the universe long ago divided and particularised itself, in order to observe and experience itself. We are all a result of that division.

The division was a terrible and irresponsible error which all competent religions have since set about correcting by attempting to re-fuse us into the all. The question is, why re-merge into something so clumsy and rash? I suspect the Errorverse has realised its error but has now convinced itself retrospectively of some other motive – to give birth to something truly separate and outside itself, perhaps. Not very likely – a true individual.'

'And then what? When this individual exists? What's his reward?'

'Nothing.' Werther's eyes filled with soft pity. 'The self-divided universe, separated to observe itself. In its jaws happiness and torment are known side by side like the seconds in a minute.'

Lit by the painful clarity of perpetual collapse, Werther stood, his funeral shape floating toward Leo. He helped Leo to his feet and wiped the ashes from his purple coat. 'Your plans are fallen in. Busy thyself with watching. It is all that's left you. How does the deterioration of a soul affect what is around it? How the deterioration of a principle in action? Ask Li Pao – though he would deny a government was ever anything *but* a tool of repression.'

'Li Pao. Where is he?'

'Beyond my tar orchard.' The spectre waved a bone-white hand back at the throne. Behind it stretched what seemed to be a graveyard studded with jet marble cones. 'Across miles of black glass detail. Through the rolling camomile of the Thousand Fathom Prairie, until you reach a sore-looking ravine. There you will find a tree, its gnarled bole like an exposed brain. Beyond this you will find a liar.'

'Thank you.'

As Leo moved to leave, Werther grasped his arm and leaned in to whisper very close to his ear. 'Over time, failure makes a structure. Any structure can be used to climb.'

Werther's skull was flaring like a bulb, a power cell of solitude.

In a bedroom of domino patterning and Russian lacquer furniture, under a dreamcatcher like a cartoon spiderweb, Regina lay in her thirteen-poster. She slept curled up like a fist, her polychroming body a writhe of streamers.

They met on the muffled strangeness of a clay promenade with off-white statues of strolling couples. A short way off, his dye-stamp feathers clinking like cutlery, Whisper Terrible seemed to be working on a medley of cloudforms. Frequencies bent across the sky as he emitted the blank whimpering and squeaks he used to communicate. He twitched his finch-like head this way and that, shivered the tines of his tail and streaked upward into the charcoal landscape of a thunderform to ride on the curled clouds. When Regina returned her gaze to earth, Leo del Toro was walking purposefully toward her down the colonnaded gallery. 'You even dream in black and white,' he said.

'I can't figure us out, Leo.'

'You think I'm a sorehead.' His face was luminant.

'This discussion again?'

He seemed amiable and amused. 'A revolutionary may not always be good – he may sometimes be merely noble.'

'What is "noble"?'

'Striving in the face of what he knows can't be changed.'

'I suppose the role has some points of interest.'

He scowled. 'It's not a role,' he stated levelly. 'And I am more than spectacle. A prisoner of a whole world is yet a prisoner, and this is no time to be neutral.'

'Comparison is disliked,' she told him, 'and, in an infinite universe, unnecessary.'

Water sounded somewhere. A long way off she could see the sentient, senile cities.

'Whatever it is you folk think you're doing out here,' he was saying, 'it's to *somebody's* cost. God knows what you've interred amidst the dead of this society ...'

He seemed, indeed, in an agony of conviction. At first she had been entertained by his complicated fury, but now felt drawn to examine it in detail, as she had seen her uncle studying the thread of filigree in some trinket from the past. Sometimes Leo swaggered his principles as if they were heavy boots giving his legs a stronger swing. He made no effort to be liked. In fact he was obliviously disagreeable, preoccupied with 'explosives' and moral arcana. She was surprised at her own patience.

'People forgive themselves too quickly,' he said now. 'Injustice past is still injustice. People forget very fast. But somewhere in time, that suffering still exists – perhaps all the more if it was never recognised or remedied.'

'Leo,' she said quietly, 'that's all very commendable I'm sure, but it doesn't sound like love.'

He was embarrassed, so he spoke sternly. 'Love is not necessarily friendly. It even affords some an opportunity to dismiss the profound.' Then he seemed to catch himself. 'I'm sorry. This is the worst of it. Not much remains for love. And then I've no idea when my visions speak through malice.'

Her eye rested upon the nearest couple of blank-eyed lovers on their pedestal. A slogan on the plinth read: *The crow's white skeleton.*

She knew at once that Leo was in a sort of disguise. The alien loftiness of his feelings, on wing in high dark, concealed the fact that he meant what he said. It was not an affectation and he would remain this way irrespective of the trend. She had never encountered such a thing. Without knowing what it was, she felt a vertiginous sense of heresy.

Leo had taken her hands folded like a pale rose and pressed them to his mouth, kissing them. His eyes were closed. 'Help me,' he whispered.

Something was exchanged, and when his hands left hers, a ring was on his finger. He turned to leave.

She tried to move and fell, finding herself locked in place. The inked vines that twisted around her body were thickened and real around her legs, arching stiffly from her feet to root her to the paving stones. She crouched, trying to break the tough black branches. Black tears began to run down her face and she heeled them away with her hands, looking around. Leo had disappeared.

Standing, she locked her arms around a stone column, and wrenched her right foot away from the ground – the roots tore like veins, spurting a shock of crimson blood which puddled outward quickly, reflecting her panicked face. Pulling at her other leg, she felt her heart begin to draw; felt the membrane tear.

Above her bed, the dreamcatcher burst into flames.

1 1

THE STRAW MAN

Showing the Truth of the Observation of Violaine
That Some Use Questions as Vessels of Disposal

Tramping across a nightmare expanse of ringing black glass, Leo blinked away a fever vision in which he tore a Band-Aid off his neck and blinding light poured out. His left hand was numb – was he about to have a heart attack? The sky was periodically charged with changes in meteorological flavour and other celestial transactions he didn't understand. It seemed sometimes heaven had a day terror, the trauma spreading. A huge sickly face blew by, denting like an escaped parachute.

By the time he was content to consider 'the next day' Leo could see in the landscape ahead of him another invented perfection. There was first a thin strip of penny-brown sand that seemed to serve as the boundary of two worlds welded together, then he waded into a pear-coloured prairie. He reached a solid silver tree, unpolished and granular. Beyond this was a tobacco-stained wall hairy with weeds. Leo went through a Moroccan archway into a new climate.

A small enamel cottage stood in a gemlike garden fizzing with insect life. The wind-shimmered peacock-green lawn sent up the fragrance of jasmine. Leo unlatched a hedge gate and walked through. The garden was designed to be both opulent and delicate, profuse with detail: fat orange roses, drooping trumpet flowers, hissing camphor and bloodgum trees, ornate cast-iron furniture starting to rust. Leo touched the cottage's cold glossy surface. The doorknocker was a single serrated pincer apparently from a large brown stag beetle. It made hardly a sound. He looked back at the garden. A golden, leaf-speckled clearing dazzled like green fire.

'Steam-engine lawn in the verde-antique style.'

Leo turned to see the speaker was an oriental gentleman in blue overalls, and lacking any anatomical extravagance. The man finished shuffling a pack of rose window playing cards and placed them into a denim pocket over his heart. 'Li Pao, Returning Executive Officer of the 27th Century People's Republic.' Then he awkwardly squeezed the door closed behind him, but not before Leo had glimpsed a gaudy world of yellow paint, banana toffee and tigers. 'And you are Leo del Toro, starter of many fires. I am honoured. Sit down here, you must be tired. Sand particles galore, yes?'

'Galore,' Leo repeated numbly, falling heavily on to the weathered oak bench which was set against the cottage wall.

The Chinese sat next to him, all attention. He seemed to study Leo intently for a time. Leo became very aware of his own exhaustion. There was a stone in his boot. He removed the boot and tipped sand into his hand, plus a diamond big as half a golfball.

Putting the diamond in a coat pocket, he pulled his boot on again. These small efforts drained him.

'You travelled here through time,' said Li Pao.

'Not in any way I understand, but yes. Accident, apparently.'

'But you are not the Duke's golem, certainly. Threshold man gone renegade, they're saying. Dawn Ages, isn't it? What century? Not the twenty-seventh?'

'Twenty-first.'

'The end of the Fourth World age, the Kali Yuga before the fourth Apocalypse of the Obvious and Intercession of the Tall Boys. Yes, you are the man I suspected you to be. An ambassador from reality, in a way.'

'What do you mean?'

'Well, you've had a taste of this chaos of conjurations, yes? This is an unvexed age, a heart which changes with every beat. Freed from necessity and material want, its people choose aimless dissolution, submission to amorous novelty and a thousand improvised histories. They are self-regarding yet without self-knowledge, minutely-appointed buffoons, capricious and absolute as Greek gods. Their women dispense with so many of the veils of romance that it leaves a man with almost nothing to do. You've probably seen some of the men playing football? Here, all is transient not through death and erosion, but through accelerated fashion merely. And the approaching End of everything, of course; but that's always been approaching hasn't it?'

'I met Mr Werther. He seemed quite anxious.'

'Ah yes, sorrowful Werther and his entertaining nostalgia for death. He's been studying sterility, of late. He's almost perfected it, I believe. Put on a show of it a while ago that almost killed the audience. Quite remarkable.'

'A show?'

'I doubt he'll stick with anything quite so dry, however. Not enough drama or thunderous wilting. Werther's actually a romantic, you see. Managing eighty cigarettes a day, I heard.'

'Yes.'

'I certainly expected nothing less. And you've met Jagged?'

Leo thought of the enigmatic Lord of Canaria. 'I can't help thinking I recognise him. From some time before, I mean.'

'It's rumoured he time-travels on occasion. Backward, I mean.'

'That's possible?'

'Opinions differ. Forward travel is possible of course, that's how you and I got here. But reverse travel is supposedly limited. Doesn't stick for long. You just get rebounded forward again.'

'Why?'

'Because forward motion is natural, and once you've gone forward you no longer belong in the past. Or so Brannart Morphail says. He named it the Morphail Effect, in the conceited way of these people. Childish nobles, they rez a desert and call it paradise.'

Li Pao slapped his hand through the trunk of a nearby apple tree, sending bubbles of it flurrying off. The gap closed up instantly. 'This is not the fruit of experience, but of quick trickery.'

Leo looked at the garden. The sun was pleasantly warm. When the breeze blew over the grass it sounded like a thousand glasses touching.

'Then you arrive,' Li Pao continued with greater weight, staring at him. 'Blowing into town to wreak seven shades of clarity on them while dumping waste irony behind you wherever you go. A firebrand.'

Leo didn't know what to make of the man's unctuous, almost gothic empathy. 'You said you knew who I was. Do these people know?'

'Oh, their notion of history is the ... ridiculously appointed counterfeit epochs they cast up for entertainment. But if I have it correct, yes, you established yourself in the pantheon, among your enemies. Young and full of ginger, you bestrode oppression with boots of steel. And I know of your climactic revolution. It led to a period later referred to as the Brief Period of Lucidity.'

'Brief?'

'Of course. Despite its apparent consolidation by a few natural disasters shortly after and the practicality they encouraged, everything returned to the usual form. People, *en masse*, had not changed. How could such a thing be expected?'

'Your people are different.'

'In a way ... but only after billions of years, a span unimaginable by the mind, and topped by the special circumstance which I assume you now understand. Longevity adds impossible compass points to their options. Anything may be instantly manifested or altered. And all will end. And really, have they changed as you would have hoped? You surely hoped for more than scene-shifters.'

He clearly knew more than he was letting on. But Leo sat absorbing what had been said. Countless revolutions had presumably been and gone. After his last one Leo had thought he might move on to another society in roughly the same jam and get organising. Evasionomics and terracidal self-blinding seemed fairly universal. But he could do nothing here. And had never, ultimately, done anything.

'Let us for a moment fantasise,' said Li Pao in a quiet, almost hypnotic tone. 'If you could do anything, what would it be?'

After Leo described, as hopefully as he could, the sort of revolution he had in mind, the other man started to allege his own beliefs. 'Rebellion as a posture delivers exquisite and obscure pleasures. Such pleasant alienation is a part of government's mildest lament – a weak shadow of the outrage and true freedom which is government's actual nemesis. Authority's ideal is to take hypocrisy far enough beyond measure that people are left behind, measuring it with their standard ruler while the hyper-hypocrisy is free to play way out on the bell curve. They're left back there rattling around within their limited conception of how far dishonesty can go. Unalloyed capitalism: an idea that is correct in the minds of its victims. It must permeate everything until people detect a transaction even in the fluffiest summer clouds.'

'True enough,' Leo said, 'and helpful to anyone wishing to set up an hegemony, but we aim to disassemble it, surely?'

'I heard about your colourful explosions. A wonderful attempt by old means, but these are new times. Perhaps you should let me do the talking from now on. Our insurrection should be scrupulously mounted. Society's padded contradictions, aged arrangements of royalty that are basically statues made of dust bonded by habit – all this to informed skeptics, realists like ourselves, is merely a shabby buttress to the cruel illusion of convention. Sometimes, you see a thing the way it really is. Sometimes you don't. Anyone who sees through their own eyes and thinks with their own brain will understand that power is a shell-game using nested dolls. Yet much of it is automated. Just because something has structure does not mean it is not dumb mass.'

'That depends on whether the structure is used to process anything – and, I'd add, what that processing is used for. I'd say it's not dumb mass, it's deliberate malice. That malice is camouflaged by the apparently dispassionate quality of disregard. But just because such processes have been inherited and systematized, doesn't mean they can't be halted or changed.'

'Precisely. So pleasant to be able to speak of these matters with one who understands.'

Leo looked at the bright flowers and observed: *simplicity does not require sincerity. Natural honesty is unaware of itself.* He noticed that Li Pao was holding a copper rosette in his hand, tapping at the petals as though at a cellphone. Tucking it away under the seat like an ashtray, Li Pao resumed his discourse. 'What's the difference, do you think, between revolution and transformation?'

Leo found the question facile. 'Decibels?'

'One is imposed by one group upon another, the other is gradual change from within. It's not hard to unglue allegiances bonded by a certain fearful greed, but that doesn't change the principle at its core. Devisers of human deceit in different camps provide the language we speak. And unanimity is a blank page upon which any outrage may be written. We must surely develop another language. A lie requires at least two people to operate.'

'Not so. One can lie to oneself.'

'Language helps there too. Ah, I've taken a liking to you, Leo del Toro. Walk with me.' They stood, and began a leisurely stroll across the garden of sensitive flames. Li Pao seemed to have planted a square of ground with very dry human bones angled like scaffolding. 'This is known as a victory garden, as you probably know. Yes, humankind is asleep. Not dreamless perhaps, but asleep nonetheless. You and I will show them a thing or two. What has gone before is badly presented prologue. That's my firm belief.'

'Your generosity is curiously contrived. And advice, in my experience, tends to absent itself before consequence comes along.'

Li Pao seemed not to hear him. 'Look at the bees and other insects, having paroxysms all over the place. That one over there landed on a flower, look, and flew off again almost instantly. Why do they do what they do? I give up.'

They passed through a gate woven from red and yellow iron, into an open grey plain.

'Your idea of revolution sounds like PR,' Leo

remarked. 'What about acting with an eye to what is right rather than what is lawful. What about awareness.'

'What's that, in the current interpretation of the word? A notion of which all other ideas are mere degenerate variants, eh? Something grand and strange, I'll be bound.'

A bony lizard rattled on a rock and then blew away in a slight breeze. They paused here.

'My dear del Toro, no enlightenment is an excuse for being stupid. In your past as I have studied it in history, these beliefs of yours were sensationalised until they were useless. Inverted substance holds on to its name, as you surely know.'

'And what has revolution become?' Leo pretended to ask.

'Time has not been kind to the concept – nor to any other. Too many snags. The matter rests in the midst of blight, regrettably. Halted by lack and emergency, as it must always be lest true progress should occur. The agitator remains merely the bitter outsider amid competing proofs.'

Leo saw the argument, its gallery of load-bearing assumptions and the emptiness around them. 'So there it is – the hopes of villains justified.'

'Oh, don't think that way. We must fight from within. Revolution is a gradual process.'

'We are at the End of Time.'

'I've made no secret of my revolutionary principles. That's bravery. I readily admit, with impossible sorcerers commonplace and apparently earnest in their views, the sentiment might be a little lost ...'

'You wear no rings. You choose to spurn such magic.'

'Well, yes,' said Li Pao, his look slightly evasive. 'Of course, many centuries must pass before a ... visitor is allowed them.'

'Visitor?'

'I told you I'm from a past age. The Duke knows I'm an intelligent lifeform and thus allowed to wander freely if I wish. He made this environment for me. But power rings are another matter.'

'Then ... you're a slave here?'

'As to "slave" ... no, I wouldn't say "slave". They would call me an exhibit, perhaps. A specimen. I allow them their illusions.'

'You aren't free?'

'Perhaps they would say, *free-range*,' Li Pao replied, adding a slight laugh as if it were a trifling matter.

'After all you've said? The beliefs you claim?'

Leo felt sick. The man's beliefs were mental decoration, not designed to be applied. They were like the motors of this age, their workings mere superfluous rites. 'A world of tears and patches – and a rebel to match.'

'You think so?' Li Pao seemed to withdraw, his face growing slack and uncaring. 'There once existed a school of oriental craftsmen who deliberately dropped and smashed their finely-wrought plates and vases, because they felt that the carefully repaired object, with its obvious cracks and joinery, was more beautiful than the original.'

'Justification.'

'You try living here, young lionheart. And vegetate with grace. All that's left to you is a docile bay and quiet years.'

A large red mantid was skimming through the air toward them.

'Go to hell.'

If Li Pao was surprised by the request he did not show it.

The giant translucent mantis deployed its landing legs and settled on the ground. Its thorax opened and Doctor Volospion walked down a thin wing, a smile on his sharp face.

12

THE HOUSE OF DEATH

Proof of the Fallibility of Religion to Disarm

The ruby insect tucked up its legs and levitated. Volospion stood unnecessarily at the tiller, feeling quite pleased with himself. He had obtained the coveted Leo del Toro. The specimen seemed rather glum, however, sitting against the shelf formed by a rear rib of the ship as the ground slanted away. Red-stained clouds and mountains curved around the cherry glass of the vehicle's thorax. 'I'm glad Li Pao contacted me,' Volospion called back at his passenger. 'Though the Chinaman can usually, as they say, "talk the ears off an otter". You have become the standard by which violent self-regard is measured.'

Passing below was a town in flames, circulated in endless terror by burning men trailing smoke where they ran. The flailing silhouettes volleyed screams of stark agony.

'What's that?'

'Tulsa Kloma 21. No-one remembers what it is or who did it, but it's there still. A startling tableau.'

'Don't you people clean up after yourselves?'

'It's without much consequence, as with everything else.'

Leo sat brooding, arms folded. Further on was a

111

forest of dry spiral candy and curved black stalagmites like towering triggers.

'This is Pompeii,' Volospion explained, 'as it appeared before Len and Trotsky knocked it down, from necessity.'

The passenger was now lambent with some interesting species of indignation, its source a mystery. Volospion was quietly fascinated.

They skimmed over a ragged phalanx of assorted alien creatures, the herd straggling in the same direction as the airbug. Between Volospion's craft and the multiform rabble flew a kind of pteranadon, its shadow rippling across the landscape. It made for an interesting effect. The glass airbug quickly left the herd behind.

Presently Volospion deployed the landing legs and brought the mantis in to land on a chalky plateau. 'I can promise,' he said, 'no such empty sybaritic diversions as you have seen from my colleagues. I participate as one must, but my deep interests lay elsewhere – or one might say I am a voluptuary of a different order. Wisdom is not contagious, and morality is not to everyone's taste.'

Without replying, Leo left the vehicle. The terrain bristled with opalescent thorns. Stone ructions were clustered in heavy waves dyed china white. Created in seconds years ago and never demolished, they had become fringed with pink weeds. 'Plants grow here?' Leo asked.

'We don't know if they happen naturally or as a result of our dreams. Many of us remove our rings when we choose to sleep, in case of unconscious projection. Werther de Goethe once infected the land with a decade of rather plain ghosts.'

'He now sleeps without his rings?'

'He now never sleeps.'

They crossed the buckled land. A tangerine rocksalt bridge joined hands over a chasm, at the end of which a polished copper tumour protruded from the valley side. 'My pavilion. No frivolity there, but high meaning on every surface. I know a man like you will appreciate it.'

They crossed the small garden where he was cultivating a plot of grail tubers surrounding an ornamental fountain spouting the blood of a giant subterranean lamb. 'These luminant pitcher plants are natural, in most respects. Man-made, but long ago.'

'That's a niceness of distinction.'

The interior space seemed to exist independently of the building's outer form. It contained a maze of arched galleries decorated with votive grenades, burnt-out church valves and other devotional gewgaws which he proceeded to show to Leo with a kind of baffled pride. All the paraphernalia of faith – though to Volospion's mind the notion that faith should require paraphernalia seemed a contradiction. There was a great deal he did not understand, and he knew it. Yet his was a dedication without ardency, and as his collection grew his comprehension did not. He was merely puzzled as to how these excavated cosmologies fit together.

He had a hinged wooden stack which unfolded to show three faded pictures of people, each with a melon balanced on their heads. A religious time traveller had told him it was an ikon and that it was holy, but Volospion still wasn't sure what it was used for. He had once conjured a melon and placed it on his head, looking at the ikon images as though into a mirror. Would this imitation instill some special feeling in him? He felt no change. He had dismissed the melon. Regarding these matters he was infinitely patient. The longer it occupied his time, the more it will have served him. He explained it now to Leo, who regarded Volospion with, apparently, a quizzical horror.

In further chambers seeded with the vintage smell of dust and dead wax Volospion pointed out undecyphered parchments and inert amulets, Tefillin pans and ecumenical firecrackers displayed on force-domed pedestals. Here were wolf tickets, a troy ounce of Eden apple tears, an owl mummy like a cocoon, a Tarot deck with the legendary extra card, a brace of rotted Vatican safety belts, the tongue of Suhulu, Gore's Harp, the glass jaw of Saint Just, two pale nephrite masks representing the sacred visages of Ashley and Stacy, a banner reading RICE TWICE, and a round Calamity Bible. Everywhere was the old crumbled plumage of uniforms and different-coloured manuals containing the procedures of messianism. Our Lady of Abraxas looked down from a framed painting. A porcelain bust of Madame Ortiz glowed from an adjacent corner. Here was a singularity zodiac, the great weight and crammed detail of which suggested it had been miniaturised from a much greater size. In a bronze sideboard he kept the *Interminabula*, summarized in thirty verdure books. 'Its sentences like the world of high branches,' Volospion told Leo, possibly quoting from somewhere (Volospion could never be sure), 'hushed through with the whisper of leaves. A secret may hide safe in it. Chattering seekers never look up.' He paused, then thought to add: 'I have learned the art of reading.'

From a corner he produced a saint's scarred suitcase. 'Bishop McCain's satchel. He sealed eighty ecstacies into his unbelief while denying them to others. Shut himself away from adoration. A special moon was reserved to signal his death. I do not think even your Mr Hitler could say as much. And over here – I believe this was once a Kleist doll, but it is inoperative. Again the Shuttle Clue says it ingested just enough knowledge to lose its "grace" and not enough to re-attain it. Does that make sense to you?'

'Yes.'

'Really? It means nothing to me. Perhaps you can explain it to me during one of our discussions.'

'Discussions?'

Without troubling to reply, Volospion directed Leo to another room, larger than the others, in which hung a faded vimana sail tattooed with the Bird Reich insignia. On the floor a blue-black mosaic of Melchizedek's galleon was at anchor. Animated tapestries of alien deities cavorted silently across the walls. Suspended on wires was a fibreglass effigy of Woon, the goddess of time. She resembled a transparent sea urchin, her spikes pointing in all directions.

Volospion arranged a Pretext Oracle and the

Cellphone of Julian of Norwich on a small god shelf and intoned flatly 'In the name of the father, the sun and the friendly ghost.' He turned to Leo. 'That was "prayer", or "conversing with the hidden citizen".' He removed a chrome disk from a trunk. 'And this is a plate from the reign of Anu.'

'That's a hubcap, Mr Volospion. From a car.'

Volospion tucked in his pointed chin, and gave a small sigh. 'So many claims upon my energies.' But he had been bluff and hearty during their romp through baked remnants and this minor disappointment did not faze him for long. Beyond this room was his small menagerie of nuns, gurus and godlets. The thought pleased him.

'I don't understand,' said his guest.

'Oh?' Volospion replied, feeling informed and efficient. 'I'll try to answer any questions you have.'

'I don't get the dime museum angle, your interest in all this. In my time knowledgeable people understood most of this was trickery and that the rare real thing was a private matter.'

'I too persist in hailing back to past trivialities, I can't help it. Most of us do, at the End of Time. It's difficult to distil new vices in such an old universe. We have a delightful hunger, and an endless one. Our distraction will never be completed.'

'The past, and truth. One thing has nothing to do with the other, except insofar as one can actually and actively learn from it. Your "history" here ... it's a guess within a guess.'

'Gods, then – they weren't a decanter in your celestial cabinet?'

Leo picked up the cardinal red skull of Kaiser Clare and examined it negligently. 'God was seen as the great anatomist madman. Its tantrums are subterfuge. How could they be otherwise, if it's all-powerful?'

'Ah,' said Volospion, and looked at Leo with new interest. 'Hearsay and heresy, then.'

'When religion responds to true humour with disapproval, we know the conclusion we must draw. A large amount of space is suddenly provided us to ignore, or perhaps to use in an interesting way.'

'I see. Yes, I think I see. You mean that what matters is our oneness with the interval.'

Leo scowled. 'I mean that "gods" build beauty into trespass and then come along blaming. This is the clue that their doctrines are actually prescribed by bodies of human authority.'

'Ah. Fascinating! But there is this risk: if we establish contradiction in the framework of a planet, where will you fasten your mind? No, let us make it all the same.'

'You completely misunderstand.'

'I do? You're right,' Volospion supposed. 'Do you want consolation? Gifts? We could start the visit again ...'

'Stop talking like that. It's doing my head in.'

'I will stop. Most natural thing in the world. Snakes crawl without a snort of triumph, after all. I shall in all things endeavor to be silent.' Volospion tossed the hubcap back into the trunk and dropped the lid closed. He turned to Leo. 'Well, it has been a pleasure meeting you. In fact, I insist you never leave.'

'What?'

'I won't ask you to remain a free man, if you don't mind. Jagged and I agreed you'd be my specimen if you proved to be of natural origin.'

Leo del Toro took the news quite badly, explaining more of his novel philosophy. Volospion thought he recognised the outlines of a rote drama and attempted to retrieve the appropriate stance from his memory. He summoned a cold look. 'You are right to be ...' he faltered. 'Afraid, is it? Of me. And now that you have completed the formalities of begging for mercy, I'll show you your new environment. It's rather spacious. And there are crystallised fruits.'

'I'm not one of your tin saints. Goodbye.'

'The outer chambers are now force-shielded. And you surely belong, resolved as you are to follow divine example. Carrying events a little further perhaps. You seem to regard yourself as the regulator of our morals. Well, an angel deprived of its wings will yet fly a while, like a chicken deprived of its head.'

Leo was weary, exasperated. 'I can't wait here with you. Your whole setup's a cliché.'

'Like an eyeball with spiderlegs, you mean?' Volospion went on in a calm, implacable voice. 'Interesting. I could offer you a talcum mine. I know how much that resource was treasured in your time.'

'Are you insane?'

Volospion became puzzled. His force barriers were being dissolved. A blue gas was coalescing in the chamber, bubbling up into a mound of eyeballs as it neutralised the final energy shield. These swivelled to Leo as one, pupils dilating. 'And not one of them has legs,' Volospion remarked, at which they instantly regarded him. But when the cloud contracted with a dull bang it appeared to have signalled a spot of uproar. A confusion of aliens assembled, filling the room with eight exotic tonnes of squelching concern. Someone was being cavalier with jellies.

Next a panther with red-gold fur walked in, its shoulders rolling, head low. 'This enslavement is dissolved,' it whispered telepathically. After some initial bafflement, the chrono-transient became traitorous and aglow.

'Struggling out loud,' Volospion chided, 'it's so uncouth.'

And now apparently nothing would do but that Leo del Toro should punch him in the face. Volospion fell crashing into a pile of canonical conceits in fuselli tin. 'You punched me,' he said, bewildered. 'I can't honestly say I enjoyed it, but I can't bring myself to resent it either. How many such blows can you manage per hour?' And as he remembered too late that manners were a cut glass portcullis too fragile for action, he saw Leo draw his arm back for another shot.

Thinking strategically, Leo decided to shorten his lines of communication by shouting point-blank into Volospion's face while striking the second blow. Then he found himself taken up on gelid shoulders and paraded out of the building, surrounded by jubilant multiforms. Dumped on the feldspar plateau, he became the focus of an eldritch expectancy that crowded about him in an amazing confusion of detail. Here was an unfathomable labyrinth of guts in a scratched Ocean Mirrors uniform, there an elegant web of nerve tissue that billowed with imperceptible breezes, and beyond them another being that was basically an upright and overjoyed anteater with leaking eyes. A crustacean like a pale hand drew near, its complicated mouthparts whirring excitedly. Another presence bloomed continually in the air like an ongoing inkblot. Still another seemed to be a set of giant flubbering tonsils. Leo's face was rippling in the flank of a cow-sized dinosaur made of flowing mercury. A carnival-patterned oyster snapped at him from the floor like a clockwork toy. Folding and waddling behind him was a pteranadon with a long stained glass forehead and skin mottled and detailed as desiccated leaves. A pitch black devil analogue with bright yellow teeth and tall sodalite horns embraced Leo and wept.

Amid this pantomimic jamboree he noticed a dolphin on training wheels and knew these were the aliens he had freed from the Iron Orchid's menagerie. Loosed from their terrariums into the equally false light of this world, they had evidently been following him for days, and wished to follow him further. They had entered Volospion's pavilion with the combination of violence and shameless wiseacreing that made it clear no long-range plan had been formed. And they seemed to have planted a chemical marker for any other stray creatures to converge upon with mandibles aquiver. Only the Napoleons were absent.

The upholstered panther strolled powerfully forward, attended by the eyeball swarm and other bantamweight enigmas. Its whispered words appeared in the centre of Leo's head. 'I am honoured to address the Lion of Fire, Chinashop Bull, Man of Anger Due to Several Perfectly Obvious Causes. Welcome on the Earth.' The aliens trilled and gurgled their greetings and the panther continued, its mouth never moving. 'I am Masha la Mash. For years we have dwelt on this planet – some wandering, others captive, all without obvious power. The lords of Earth live in structures without foundation and amuse themselves by harassing and detaining aliens and time travellers. We know of your seditions, fine judgement and economy of action. Even had we not already been so inclined, you have made a good case for rebellion and shown us the honour of the act, even when futile. Naturally the matter outweighs galactic rivalries. We have reached an understanding on this. Thus our strange lives are in your hands.'

Sitting on a boulder, Leo set himself to consider the problem. These aliens were framing themselves as his responsibility by virtue of his having freed them. He wasn't biting. He had experienced the same moves often enough to get a feel for the way persuasion was positioned. But the fact remained, he wished to help them anyway. How? Things worked differently here, and he worked not at all. This ineffectuality had reduced him to the level of an adolescent, an untried fantasist, silly because he could no longer demonstrate a proof. Strategies discarded around him like spent bullets, he sat in recollection of more successful furies. The wheeled dolphin regarded him with flat dollar eyes.

Standing, Leo described the exploded governmental palace to the pteranodon, who recalled a landmark something like it and described its location to his colleagues. As the aliens bugged out around him, Leo mounted the pterosaur's back and the flexing creature pitched itself from the cliff edge, catching an updraft and soaring into a sky cloudy as an x-ray. The convocation of aliens dwindled behind them, faces upturned.

DAY OF THE LORDS

Which Treats of Faddish Matters

Sharp air carved past the reptile's head and seared Leo's face. The surface under his hands was lightly fuzzed like the skin of dead banknotes and he kept losing the loose scruff that was the only handhold on the creature's back. Far below passed whorled temples, awe refineries and the skeletons of rotting carousels. A herd of mechanical trilobites upholstered in burgundy leather was crossing a sheer plain of stainless steel. Until at last the palace hove up ahead. The shattered dome and ruptured land had healed over as though nothing had happened. The flying reptile gave a throaty bark as they approached the high walls, and slowed itself with panting wings to settle on a projecting vain. Leo dismounted, placing a silencing finger to his lips as the pteranadon shuttered its wings like leather fans and waddled after him to an arched embrasure.

Leo found himself looking down upon the reconstituted conclave chamber where he had earlier made his feelings clear. He was perhaps a hundred feet above a confused conference of delegates, and there were more flags and swags than ever. Absently stroking the pterosaur's great canoe of a head, he crouched listening to a combination of bizarre form and precise punctilio.

It seemed the notion of empire was losing its flavour.

Attended by deputies and subalterns, the Iron Orchid was taking her turn enthroned as the great martinet Emperor Odds. But her patience was fraying. 'My jaws and arms ache. And the outrage muscles behind my eyebrows. Finding something to interfere with every day – to be honest, it's exhausting. I think I may have got the entire motivation wrong.'

'It is a hard one to understand,' Bishop Castle conceded. 'I confess I do not entirely grasp it myself. Policy is stated but in practice surmised anew each day.'

'Well, I am tired with devising enormities,' the Orchid resumed. 'I am authorised to do ample justice to every villain but myself, apparently.'

'Unbelievable wavering!' squealed Corporal Pork.

'Quiet!' snapped Brannart Morphail, quite immersed in his role. 'Our leader will be sharing more discomfort at any minute.'

'This from one who keeps his wings in a safe.'

'Brannart's wing tragedy is not your affair, Corporal Pork,' stated the Orchid. 'And he has the only operational beard in the room. Greed finds me president, and I decree -' She raised a staff surmounted by a trumpet flower, then gave up, lowering it. 'I don't know.' She looked around at the banners, blazons and pendants Principal Krill had raved about. It seemed everyone had to have a standard of their own now.

Some even had a simple rendering of Leo del Toro's face on their flag. Others had his visage branded into the cloth of their costumes. But what did it mean? 'And so what, really, if they are inaccurate creations or tiresome originals?'

Brannart Morphail stumped forward, emphatic and stern. His hair was gathered into a topknot perpetually burning with an apple-green flame. 'Well for my part, to sheer simple fact I offer my devotion: there.'

'Meaning what exactly?' demanded Bone Quixote from atop his skeleton horse.

'We have a government and the treasure trousered thereby. What we do not have is force, its clawed relation shedding blood to fulfil its promises. Laws are backed by violence. Why else would anyone obey them?'

'Out of reasonableness?' the Orchid ventured.

'When they are backed by *violence*?' Brannart scoffed.

'We have sentries, Brannart,' said Bishop Castle. Here and there stood a few bored and floundering enforcers in atrocity vests.

Brannart announced his intention to bray with laughter, and then did so. 'Them? Who will coach and drill them? We need an army, a disaster in keeping with the general tone of our enterprise. And here is Lord Shark the Unknown, whom I invited to keep our troops in fighting trim. Come, Lord Shark: ingratiate yourself into the normal flow of society.'

The assembly parted as a figure in a grey claw-hammer coat strode across the chamber. His head was occluded by a metal mask in the shape of a shark's gaping maw. He stopped before the throne, nodded sharply at the disguised Orchid, and gave his attention to the dwarfish scientist Brannart Morphail.

'All ears as usual, eh Shark?'

'I suppose your remark has meaning,' said the grey Lord Shark without interest.

'I've discovered that sharks were made entirely of cartilage, the stuff of which the human ear is also constructed. You are all ears, oh dreamless one.'

Lord Shark stood silent and immobile, his red eyes glowing within the jawed helmet.

'And they had no visible ears, of course,' Brannart continued. 'That was always the main trouble with sharks – impossible to know where the nose ends and the body begins.'

'Hard to know where to kiss the brute,' Bishop Castle chipped in.

'Exactly,' Brannart smiled.

Lord Shark nodded sharply at the disguised Orchid, turned, and strode out of the chamber, the assembly parting and closing again.

Brannart sighed. 'Ah, such a solitary fellow. I suppose we shan't see him for another hundred years or so.'

'Prince Ozay's the same,' said the Orchid, then slapped her knee, deciding. 'As for the throne, I've been transfixed by its various permutations for days now, and it is time to move along.' She stood and Emperor Linden Odds fell away – she was herself, draped in streams of black and purple pearls like a god widow. 'Who will "mount the ignored rostrum" next? Where is Volospion?'

'I believe he visits Quoi Vico the Fob, whom Werther mentioned. He thinks the clockmaker can mend his spiky brain.'

The hulking Baron Coma stepped forward, without interrupting his knitting of a flag banded in colours toxic as tropical insects. Tucked beneath his short knotted horns was an ornamental frown. 'I speak for many when I say I have gloried in empire. But the swoon of our days – it falters. Cut up by del Toro's terms.'

'I agree,' bleated Brannart Morphail. 'This rampaging primate of opinion – *opinion*, mind you – and his ungovernable temper, provide the whip-thin argument for war we require. Laws clothe assault. Our soldiers will tear him limb from limb – and a man hates that.'

'Should we kill him, then?'

'Yes. Often.'

'Hold hard,' someone ordered from the rear of the chamber. The enigmatic Lord Jagged of Canaria walked across the pink quartz floor, pushing before him a sort of giant gourd on a trolley.

'What's this?' asked Bishop Castle.

'This is Again the Shuttle Clue. He can't decide what to be at the moment but he wanted to enjoy the party so he's come along as some kind of chrysalis.' Jagged rapped his knuckles on the pupa and shouted, 'Isn't that right, Clue?' There was a short pause as he listened. 'He's not in a talkative mood.' He parked the trolley near the throne and then sat in the gilded seat as if merely resting his bones. 'Now, my dear

Orchid, clever Brannart, all my friends, are you not entertained by Leo del Toro?'

'His eagerness I understand,' said the Orchid, 'more or less. It has to do with curiosity and excitement at the possibilities of a changed world. But how all the anger fits in I really don't see.'

'Aren't you bothered by his zeal, Jagged?' asked Bishop Castle.

'It's not contested terrain, and he enjoys it. He even has his followers.' Jagged gestured a yellow-silked arm toward several 'courtiers' who had adopted the Leonian style of helm-like stubble and who brandished replicas of the del Toro spider-bursting 'gun'.

'As to them,' remarked Baron Coma, not looking up from his knitting, 'ask them what they believe and brace yourself for a storm of perplexity.'

'Well, gentlemen,' said Jagged mildly. 'You have heard what music gets a statue nodding inanely to itself. Yet I think del Toro teaches us more. He took the thoughtful precaution of being ineffective, after all. While instructing us that oscillations in fashion can include the incendiary. And that money was once thought the master molecule of life. Currency held almost talismanic importance for them, it seems.'

'Can we not accept,' cried Bishop Castle, 'we don't know what we're doing and have done with it? We've tried for consistency and there can't ever have been any!'

'Precisely,' Jagged stated with the ghost of a smile. 'We've had an illuminating and novel interlude, and we have Leo del Toro to thank for it. But time and fashion move on. The grass of our devil has turned brown. We require another.'

'With all speed,' added the Iron Orchid. 'This elaborate candour of yours fries my brain and, I'm sure, the brains of us all.' The Orchid turned to the others for support and, somewhat startled, they then nodded vigorously.

'Mine's toasted,' offered Bone Quixote.

Leo sat back from his vantage in the eaves. 'Plum-coloured guns? They misunderstand everything.'

Yet there was no conscious cruelty here. No framework, in fact, for cruelty. They seemed to him now both marrowless and innocent.

'You are yesterday's man.'

Leo whirled at the voice – Lord Jagged was stood on the jutting stone vain with the pterosaur, his yellow draperies flourishing in the wind. Leo peered back at the throne room – Jagged had vanished from there, teleporting instantly.

'New splendour is already cooking behind their foreheads.' The oblique Lord stroked the reptile's flank. 'I thought we might pay my castle a visit. Zinn here can come along if she wishes.'

14

THE MASTER OF THE ARCANES

*A Dialogue Between Lord Jagged and his Guest
Concerning Power*

Jagged's castle looked like a fat copper cage abandoned on the red mesa. What size of bird it could hold was beyond Leo's imagination, but Zinn immediately elected to rejoin her alien friends and guide them to the meeting place. She flapped away, trumpeting.

Over the entrance arched a perhaps nonsensical inscription in cuneiform glyphics, and then Leo found that the towering cage contained twists of impossible architecture invisible from outside. He followed Jagged through passages of yellow and orange tesserae and into a triangular salon carpeted with the eyelashes of a million angels, probably artificial. A banana tree grew at the room's centre and around this midrib turned a spiral staircase of green iron. On recessed shelves were specimens of the eleven branches of misdirective art. Leo noticed bone miniatures, woodcuts carved from cherry root, an opera glass, a judge's scalp, Thai kettle guns, bowls of liverworts and mosses, Egyptian ochre wine and galleon spices. In one corner a little blue glass fountain was playing, in another a five-footed gold glass urn from which lime-green flowers overflowed, and in the third a statue of a small-breasted water-nymph emerged from the floor in a diamond spume. A skylight of yellow citrine stained the chamber. Jagged regarded a rich mosaic in the New Persian style, apparently portraying Bruce Dern attacked by flying ants. 'You have followed the olvis stone road a long way,' he said. 'You are entitled to an explanation.'

'I suppose this is another of your performances.'

Jagged turned, looking slightly surprised. 'Not at all.'

'You know I blew you to pieces once, I can do it again.'

'As often as you like, dear fellow. Sit down.'

They sat in wing armchairs fashioned from remelted lava, and Jagged poured tea. The Lord of Canaria sat with an easy dignity. Leo was uncomfortable. He saw on the small milk quartz coffee table a 20th century *Journal de Tanger* in mint condition.

'I served this tea many years ago to Ambrose Bierce.'

'Ambrose Bierce the writer?'

'Ah ... well, yes.'

'Where is he? Is he still here?'

'No, he went into space with a few friends.'

'He must have hated it here.'

'Oh no, he was having the time of his life. More and more these days I find myself remembering it.'

They drank heart-root tea amid the curios and ornaments and the scent of lemon-oil furniture polish.

'You and I are like-minds, in a way. Curious about

the wiring under the boards. And perhaps carrying out a bit of rewiring.'

'I'm not so furtive as all that. We're not alike.'

Jagged frowned, considering how to proceed. 'Let me explain something to you. There is a reason for our fancies, our collections, and our interest in the past. Fancies cast out of whole cloth tend to a thinness, a lack of substance and no real focal point. The past provides fuel for our invention. But there are limits to what we can learn from relics. No honour among fossils. Yet when any of us attempt to reproduce some true work of art from the past, merely from the idea of it, the result is a generalised travesty. Even travellers from the past who have seen a great painting first-hand find they cannot power one up from the image in their minds – it comes out a sort of smudge, no detail. Still, when time travellers crash to earth here, by mishap or otherwise, they are cherished. You may find our interest shallow, but it is genuine. A mind can grasp samples. We may try to measure space, after all, though space exists beyond all measure. We cope by measuring just a small sample of it. Of course, true perspective imparts no calumnies – it offends only by truth, and by the fact that we err from it.'

'But you try. At least you yourself try, in small measures.'

'Yes. And I care about what is learned.'

'Why? When you know everything will end. Humour me with an answer.'

'Perhaps it only boils down to appetite. Perhaps I delude myself that it matters. But I feel, yes, I *feel* that it has inherent value, in this moment, and in this, and in this.'

'I see.'

Jagged seemed to have an inspiration. 'Your yearning for "justice" is perhaps anchored in the same way.'

'It hasn't been anchored since I arrived here. How could it be?'

Lord Jagged thought about it, then stood. 'Let me show you something.'

He took from an alcove a book bound between two orangewood boards, as Leo joined him. 'You were a name for several decades. Here's a picture of you with a shirt wrapped around the top of your head. Eh?'

Leo grunted.

'It was … what was it?' Jagged flicked through history, finding the page. '"A life of wretchedness and resolution. Strength and lament." Barred from life by an apparently insurmountable honesty – that was the story in retrospect. And it says: "In the presence of injustice his seditious nature revealed itself like security paint under fluorescent light." That's not bad, is it? You disappeared before you could become entirely your opposite. And your image became iconic, instantly recognisable.'

'Is that all. Where are my lieutenants? What did they think happened to me? Did they think I abandoned them?'

Leo fell into one of the chairs. Ever since he had been magicked here and met with welcome, integration and contentless understanding – followed by a bland lip-service to him as a worn-out fad – he had been confounded. For days now he had been feeling the almost-forgotten cramp of childhood, that combination of sourness and postponement. Thwarted.

'Most who claim rebellion are stupefyingly innocuous,' Jagged continued, sitting opposite and taking up his tea again. 'You spent years choking on the ashes of your enemies. But I should have known that such passion, dropped here, would spread too thin to persist. Now tell me something: Leo del Toro returns from the desert with a halo of answers. What happened? Speak of the revealed world.'

Leo gave a quick and fairly honest account of his travels and encounters.

Jagged nodded, with a slight smile. 'Werther – to cope and fade, that's his life. Though for him it is a rather playful despair. Mock dejection insults true misery, I think. Li Pao – militance turned to jelly is the weakest there is, if the militance is all the person had. No imagination, no independent thought, no true love. Anybody that worn-out carries capitulation like a credit card.'

'What do you know about credit cards?'

Jagged seemed not to hear. 'And sardonic Volospion and his wonder rooms of consecrated trinkets. Even his decency is a fanaticism, not a natural state. But – Leo – do you know why these are not people to be hated? Because it is all utterly transparent. And they know it is. A strange kind of honesty, yes, a weary kind – but what would you have, a cryptic final millennium or one with all laid bare?'

'It's no kind of honesty at all. You befoul yourselves with plastic. What good are you? What do you have to be proud of?'

'We are unexploited.'

'You exploit yourselves. Devalue. It's your only means of motion.'

'Have you spoken to Regina Sparks in these terms?'

'Yes, I suppose. I feel that her difficulties are not less than mine.'

'Thanks to you, that's becoming the case.'

'A little anguish will do her no harm atall.'

'Do you understand that she wasn't born or created here? She fell into this world through a time anomaly, years ago. She was an infant. The Duke, who is the kindest man I know, volunteered to raise her. After years in our sunlight, what can she be blamed for? You rail at her. Baffled as to what she has done wrong, she offers a prismatic contrition which touches upon a hundred likely crimes. Isn't this arrogance on your part?'

'The recognition of justice, and of the pain in the empty space between it and the world. No.'

'Have you not observed that, no matter what system they thrive or suffer with or under, a vast majority will always group into a co-conforming mass?'

'Yes, but what's the benefit of this blandness, if not just the profit of a few?'

'To maintain a consensus on the form into which we collapse the wave function. If absolutely everyone saw things differently, the world would become total variegation without duplication – chaos.'

'Interesting,' Leo mulled. 'In other words.'

'Of course, you're ungovernable. And ineffectual, thankfully.'

'Then I'm nothing.'

'You're free.'

'No. Not if I truly affect nothing.'

'Has it not occurred to you that the only way the universe will allow you to be free is if you affect nothing? Brannart Morphail has a theory on that. Time travel is like certain forms of kindness. The trick is to find a way so frail it cannot be barred, and to tread lightly.'

'What do you mean, "what the universe will allow"? And the effective people who've lived – none of them have been free?'

'Who on Earth are you referring to? And who can say? Nothing is permanent.'

'Semantics. You waste my time. Answer me without dissembling, if you're capable of it. Why am I here?'

'I can tell you exactly. The crowns and trifles we collect: what if one were able to actively pull objects and people from the past – even with some precision? These objects around us – other than their style, do they appear particularly aged?' Jagged took a last sip of tea and placed his cup down. 'And you – do you appear several hundred million years old? Why would you? You travelled here in a matter of minutes, seconds, subjectively. I brought you.'

Leo was standing, a yellow emotion fizzing where his head should have been. Jagged also stood, around him ancient appointments doubly forgotten and somehow doubly dead in their present salvation. Leo felt electricity flushing up his arms toward his heart. Jagged frowned, suddenly attentive – he seemed sharply aware of a dangerous imminence.

'I'm sorry,' Jagged said now, with a studied smoothness. 'I shouldn't have told you that way.' He took Leo gently by the arm, and Leo felt a subtle calm emanating from the erudite man. 'I shouldn't have brought you here at all. I apologise. You need some air – the dorsal door of this room leads to an observation platform.'

He guided the numb Leo up the iron stair helix. The skylight irised open and they emerged on to a railed roof atop a golden conning tower. Around and below this promontory stretched a tableland like Mars, the air aswirl with reddish sulphate dust. Directly in front of them was a sunset in dull safety orange.

'You've killed me,' said Leo. 'I'm held in suspension here. I breathe neither in nor out. It's a trap.'

'How can limitless power be a confinement?'

'When combined with limited imagination and no consequence, I suspect it's hell. And very repetitious.'

'It *is* hell,' Jagged conceded, 'for you. I should have realised that. But you presented such a possibility for learning! And for genuine belief and passion! These things are rare to us.'

'Handling a diamond makes a small mind smaller.' Leo looked fiercely into the turncoat sky. 'What, if anything, do you believe?'

Jagged answered softly, 'I believe the body was created by the heart.'

'Time's being wasted here. It's a chess game set up to absorb me.'

'I know a way through it. Carve your pawn a crown. Take power.'

'No. I refuse to indulge this counterfeit world any further. It's nothing but a pack of canards!'

'Well then go where your actions matter. I can take you there. The time device is an Absquatulata Valve, in an antechamber under Principal Krill's abode.'

Leo started away down the steps.

'Don't you trust me?' Jagged called.

'No.'

'Why not?'

'Because your neck isn't in my collar.'

Leo ran through a tangle of corridors, crossing perspex bridges and platforms from which he glimpsed Castle Canaria's vaulted ceiling of yellowed glass like the roof of a railway terminal. Finally he emerged into the almost-darkness of open air, his boots gritting on sand.

A flame approached him. It was Regina Sparks in 2012 jeans, her flesh shot through with peacock fantail eyes in double-contrast acid sapphire and chromatic mint green, carousel gold loops of gears and zodiacs in voodoo purple. Orchid scrolls and oriental pink seashells wheeled across her shoulders and bitter lemon and atomic tangerine sunsets were traversed by tiger-skinned wasps. Rose-orange flames threw cobalt shadows against a carousel pink sky between her breasts. Flames of firebrick, coral yellow, cyan ghost and reef rose spiralled around her. Overlapping silhouettes created a saturation of honeydew melon, nutmeg and pomegranate without rhyme or reason. Her great blot of a mouth was red; her hair dark blue.

'What happened,' Leo asked her, breathless.

'You ... made me blush.'

'It's good.'

'How are you?'

'I've been purified.'

'How?'

'By disgust.'

It began to rain as he ran his hands over her newly Sistine skin.

TO THINK OF TIME

Containing an Apology for the Disdainful Manner
of Doctor Volospion

Whisper Terrible was launching one of his all-over symphonic weather systems. Whisper rarely announced the unveiling of a project but kicked it off unexpectedly, sometimes overlapping upon others' concepts. They had often had to speak to him about it.

The running lights of the airbug beamed pixelating strips through the rain as Volospion landed in the Town of the Ford of the Hurdles. He descended the wing ramp, hunching his sharp shoulders against the storm. The city was creaking with corners, clotted in darkness. Volospion looked up at a tilted tower which stuck out like a bone. Disorientated, he searched again for the light he had seen from the aircar. His recent skirmish with reality had left him shaken. Those punches – outrageous. And sudden!

There was the light. A lopsided shop of timber was fronted with a large round window displaying three stark white boxes, each set with their own dark portals.

Volospion knocked at the loose wooden door and pushed in to black remains and the stink of wet charcoal. The room was cluttered with timepieces.

Some were sat back, others leaned aside. Some sounded like the tapping of a branch on a window, others like the drawing and undrawing of a doorbolt. The floor was littered with onion-skins, sand and glass glintings. Here and there ceramic pots caught the water which dripped from the ceiling – some of what Volospion had thought the ticking of ancient machinery was actually the regular plopping of water. A drenched man in a pear-brown frock coat sat on a wooden chair, tinkering with a miniature constellation of counterweights.

'You are Quoi Vico?' Volospion asked uncertainly.

The white-haired man remained focussed on his work. His head seemed to be the size of a baby's. 'Buck Whaley, Strongbow, the Fob – I have been called all these things in error. Yes, my name is Quoi Vico.'

'I am Doctor Volospion.' He gazed around him. 'Is this disorder necessary?'

'It is *order*, Doctor Volospion – natural order. And it is entirely necessary.'

'Is that a crab on the wall?'

'Sit you down, Doctor, and tell me your woes.'

As the horologist gestured to another chair, Volospion noticed he had an ornate fobwatch face set into the palm of each hand. Volospion sat and removed his steeple-crowned hat. A diamond chandelier sang with dripping rain.

'What brings you to the Hospital of Clocks? You wish to partake in the noble art of money trade? I accept pounds, tally sticks, shekels, gorees and Fox Grave's famous glass coins, if you can find any.' Quoi

Vico closed the shell of the device he held and set it down – it hatched legs and scuttled away under some sodden trash. When he looked directly at Volospion at last he had a kindly face, lined like exposed grey tree fibres. His single central eye was round, blue and clear. 'I flooded the place the other day,' he said. 'I've been experimenting with how different things look underwater. Thoughts also. And people. You should have seen Gaf the Horse in Tears when he found himself suddenly underwater in the middle of a conversation about his nose. My Orpington hens learned to fly underwater like sunfish. And observe this ancient manuscript – soaking in water has caused the words to stretch and sag. I believe the text has been translated into another language. We need merely to find the aliens who write in such a way, and what a strange masterpiece we will hear! And now, of course, this rain – just as the house was drying out. It's Whisper Terrible, I suppose?'

'I suppose also. I am tempted to visit him at that huge blue egg of his.'

'The one trembling forever on the lip of a waterfall? Is that his home? I had no idea. It's well made and pretty.'

'I agree, it is.'

'Now – what can I do for you?'

'I'm strangely troubled, and have been ever since the Duke of Queens's party the other week. Were you there?'

'No, but I heard about it. Some sort of ziggurat, and some shouting.'

'Exactly. At the end a visiting preposteror decided

to improve the shining hour by disparaging everyone and stabbing the Duke. From that day I have found myself short of patience, desirous of attention and exercising an increasingly panoramic sarcasm upon those who have no real appreciation of it.'

'Are you annoyed at the Duke or anyone else at the party?'

'I don't see why,' said Volospion vaguely. 'Jagged and I had a bit of a falling out, I suppose, seventy or so years ago, about … root babies? Root beer? Or was it the ability of stones to panic? I'm sure they never do. It's an article of faith with me even now, so perhaps that was the argument. I don't remember. Well, I have heard it said that to forget is healthy.'

'Yet you recall *that* dictum. Is it better to forget entirely, to keep memories close, or within but at a distance, thus storing away Furies to be released incensed all the more at the delay of their vengeance?'

'You are asking? I'm sure I don't know.'

'Whatever circumstances amended your views, those views are valid, so long as such circumstances exist. Reality doesn't decay.'

'Its appurtenances alter.'

'That's quite true. And the ancient soul of a wrong – this may harbour vintage truths.' Quoi Vico paused, seemingly in thought. There was so little light here, when he looked downward his eye was extinguished. Volospion glanced at the near wall, rills of water twitching across its surface. Clocks looked back at him. The pendulum of one resembled a huge scissor syringe. Another's face was set with the Purple Alphabet.

'Some say time goes in cycles,' Quoi Vico piped up, and pointed at his cyclops eye. 'But I live in the eternal present. Wherever I go I am surrounded by the dial of my directions. Time wrinkles as it ages, changes in fashion folding closer together, memory getting shorter – until all rots and sludges into spacetime paste. The same light on everything. No bit of time is superior. All that has existed exists. For you, a gap is felt between the moment and the future, but the future flows under your feet like the road under a car.'

The old man leaned aside and picked up a nugget of amber with a watch caught inside. He used it to indicate the clocks around him. 'These fabulous devices evolved from primitive sand timers after emerging onto land. They survived even the age of dinosaurs. Apparently those scaly beauties were almost constantly bellowing with anger, making the Jurassic one of the noisiest epochs this planet has been forced to endure.' He dropped the amber lozenge into a black metal grinder and began turning the handle. 'There is an old saying,' he said. '"All wounds come out in the wash." Do time and history exist in the unconscious, do you think?'

'Memory does, certainly.'

'And how long is your memory, Doctor? Even our depths have a surface, the superficial, our little circumstances. I specialise in reconciliation. All it requires is time. In the Dawn Age the passage of time brought the death of generations and much forgetting. Now it brings some forgetting – and in a world where anything is possible for anyone, that's enough.'

Quoi Vico removed the powder cup from the grinder and, peeking at the glassy dust inside, stood and took it to the square white cousin clock behind him – a device similar to the three on display in the window. He poured the contents into the powder tray and pushed it home. The clock began to hum, quantum foam tumbling in its face. Quoi Vico sat back down as though possessed of creaking old bones. 'Tell me, Doctor, what's the most recent dream you remember? Reply with sufficient manliness please.'

'Well, a while ago I dreamed I was raised from the dead, went to a party, chatted with a sort of ballistic minstrel, found some elaborate ornamentation on the fantail of the sky barge, which proved to be dozens of small purple lungs. My entire head contracted into a nest of suspicion. Then there was a long roll of thunder which became boring very quickly, but I had a blinding illumination, the feeling of which is of course difficult to describe now, that cats are the head of a shrill hurricane dialogue proceeding throughout history. Well, it seemed potent at the time. Then there was a squelch of tongues and I took it to mean I should gather up some copper-coloured monkeys that were capering around, and put them in a white cage. I struck a match and it turned into a banana, flapping open. Stood there holding it like a fool. Of course I ended up eating the thing, and was glad.'

'Interesting. What do you think it means?'

'It doesn't mean anything. It's an exact replay of what I'd done the previous day.'

'Interesting. Others have dreams and then set about creating them in life.'

'I have little imagination, Quoi Vico. I think this is why I collect religious artifacts. They combine fanciful beauty with a sort of symbolic meaning.'

'What meaning, exactly?'

'Well, all sorts. It usually involves a god or godling, and some rules or commands.'

'You've lost me I'm afraid.'

'I know, I hardly understand it myself. It's similar, I suppose, to the scenes Jagged and I have been acting out for the Duke after his gold pyramid display. But the given justification is different. Yet you know, there's something about the Duke's party ...'

Quoi Vico leaned forward. 'Yes?'

Volospion frowned, confused, then gave up. 'Oh I don't know. I suppose it's hopeless.'

'Do you remember ever having a dream, in the past, similar to the Duke's party?'

Volospion thought about it, stroking his pointed chin. 'Yes, in fact. I recall a dream I had a century or so ago in which I created a golden pyramid, very like the Duke's.'

'In which case you must have actually done so the day before.'

'Good heavens!' Volospion had a seizure of extreme awareness. He stood, his eyes pinned open. He really had created a pyramid, more than a century ago. Everyone had admired it. There had been a party. And as he remembered now, his golden pyramid had been covered in goldfish scales, and over time the scales whitened and flaked, a marvellous effect. Forgotten by all – himself included. No wonder he was bitter at the good Duke's success. 'After all,' he said aloud,

'I'm only flesh and blood, as far as I know.' He was delighted. 'You have my gratitude, Quoi Vico. I shall apologise to the Duke at once!'

Quoi Vico called after Volospion at the door. 'Doctor! Don't you have something to ask me?' He tapped his wrist.

'Eh?' Volospion turned. 'Ah yes. What, er ... "What is the time?" Is this the phrase?'

'Perfect. And the time is ...' Quoi Vico looked at the roiling face of the clock he had set humming. 'One of rare questioning. Precisely!'

THE FAITH HEALER

*Containing Great Variety of Matter, With Extraordinary
Instances of Transformation*

'When you were in the desert, I had a dream. The words inside it shouldn't have made sense to me but they did. And you were there, and Whisper Terrible, and I gave you a ring, and then I ... tried to free myself?'

The swan boat drifted over its reflection, sometimes curving its long white neck to drink from the river. Stretched out in its creamy bower, Leo and Regina drowsed in each other's arms. They breathed in one-another under the chemical-blue sky of a ballistically hot summer. Sleep would come and go like a silk curtain in a warm breeze, the fizzing of dragonflies and the gulping barks of wallet frogs blurring into dream voices.

'What did you say?' Leo asked, his voice thick.

Scrolling steadily past, the riverbank glittering with palm sugar bore nerve orchids, cabbage roses, lotus leaves and the scent of spikeward. Every blade of grass was a different shade of green. This custom tributary existed only within glance of their downy ship, fading out a little way in front and behind. Regina was adequately pleased with its high-resolution brambles and other earth ornaments. But something unusual had happened. Exposed, her beliefs had oxidised. Leo was her silent undoing, a strange and delicious downfall. This happiness, she found, had a degree of pain. The feeling, like a gas in her throat, made her feel she had to act. She didn't know what the act was yet – this present state was only half of something. She had been almosting for days, a leaf about to detach. Suspended in an alien astonishment. A golden-white singing joy in her stomach which stopped her breathing. She realised she hadn't breathed for perhaps a week. 'Is Denial like this?'

'Eh?'

'Your home – Denial.'

'Maybe it is. Look at me.'

She turned to him, the green rose vines on her neck twisting.

She smiled and then so did he. 'Good.' He kissed her, and she lay back again.

Watching the slow passing of some small star-shaped flowers, Leo felt himself nourished by gradual degrees. Clouds of drifting dandelion seeds were reflected in clear water smooth as emerald, and it seemed a delirium containing every flavour and sensation of powerful reassurance. In the midst of living white pillows Leo and Regina had dined on gums and fruits and drunk mulled lilac wine. Leo had looked in fascination at the plump segments of an orange for what seemed like days but was in fact merely three hours. And now he lay with his entire world filled with the pores of her skin, big as the bark of a tree. Heaven was in the close warm hairs on the back of her neck. Heaven was in her heart. He was always amazed that the best feelings could be so simple. It was truth like licking a stone. It simplified his reflexes. It was consoling; possible. The swarm of his worries escaped him and dispersed – gone. She turned around in his arms, facing him. She was not close enough, though he could feel her smile, feel her frown.

'Closer.'

'Sleep, and I will wind you in my arms.'

Presently, the swan ran aground on a sandbar. It had come to rest in the shadow of the Imperial Palace. Leo and Regina stepped off on to the rusty plain. Regina wiped her mouth with the back of her hand, blew up at her blunt-cut hair and turned a power ring, demolishing the swan and its attendant summerscape.

The aliens were waiting for Leo. The pterosaur Zinn was there, angling its chevron skull and oiling its wings with a tongue like a bookmark. A shellfish with eyes like knuckles and a mouthful of brushlike fibres advanced and retreated repeatedly, propelled by pulsing cilia. A tangle of sculpted scars juggled internally with its own heart. A pile of glittering lava bore slowly tumbling rubies in its pyroplastic anatomy. What had looked like a black umbrella blowing across the mesa was really a huge quick spider, sizzling like tar. A scorpion the size of a folding sofa rattled its rear. Other creatures, lacy and viscous, billowed in the warm breeze. Now they all faced forward in churchyard resignation, ready for Leo's direction. From the pantheon stalked the roiling red velveteen panther, Masha la Mash. Behind her walked a complicated coat of arms nine feet high, its openwork biology evidencing a quickened heart rate and firing synapses. Masha stopped, framed against this facade like an emblem. 'Not every dream draws from human veins, Mr del Toro,' the panther whispered in Leo's thoughts. 'Do you have anything to offer us?'

Leo was about to speak, then closed his mouth. He looked up at Odds's palace, then thoughtfully wandered toward it, regarded all the way by compound eyes.

He went inside. The deserted audience hall, devoid even of authentic memories, was beyond barren. He had felt certain the triple spine of civilisation was illusory. There was one spine: greed. The rest was simply mapped on later. Capitalism, so much lower in the food chain than luck. Dialism and its smugness, effectively nebulous. Purported communism and its very human incompetence, humourlessness and oppression; its tendency to eliminate what was good from before and to recreate what was bad in barely altered guise. But what did it matter what name was given to the system? The one continuity was the human species, which did not stop circling in the malice of its power plays. Whatever structure arose was used for this.

But at the End of Time there were no institutions, no con-game shells for today's human hermit crabs to inhabit. And when they tried to imitate those structures, like this imposter empire, it didn't stick.

They were like children, but not wantonly cruel. Lacking nothing materially, what did they lack that prevented them from re-seeding evil anew?

And he realised he had never seen them exhibit fear. When he thought of it it was like a stone hit him in the centre of the forehead.

He re-emerged into the sunlight.

Regina stood hipshot, her hands in the back pockets of her 2012s. 'Will you feed them?'

'I'll do better than that.'

Patterns criss-crossed his mind, his head rattling like a spraycan. Blood-red mischief and hope schematics created a circuit like the warm humming colours inside a perfect machine. He was fluorescing. He looked out of accelerating colours at Regina and said, as if delivering his last communication: 'Believe it hot, sacred in your stomach, like the fire of something stolen.'

He moulded his left fist into his right palm and felt a vertigo of power, his body a shaft of solid illumination. The sky recoiled. Something formed up like an ingot fallen free of the sun, and became fastened to the firmament. At first quivering like a bug in a twanged web, it stilled to the form of a banded ball. Continents were still burning to life on the sphere. And as the celestial body's arched radiance faded, the new moon presented itself as clearly lobed like the bell of a jellyfish.

Leo stood in a mist of hot vapour. His left hand was on fire. He looked at it as if in a dream, moved it back and forth, hearing it tear and sputter. Then he clenched his fist and it snuffed out.

The aliens were gone.

Leo looked up at the ridiculous thing he had cast. It was a planet segmented like an orange, each segment a different environment and home to a different species. The aliens twitched across its surface like microbes.

Fireseeds were dying in the dirt around Leo. He turned to Regina, who seemed bewildered. 'What? Not pleased I've joined you at last?'

She was looking at him strangely, her face twisted like cloth.

'Gina?'

'Leo, you don't understand. You have no power rings. How did you do that?'

He had already torn a strip off his pants leg and wrapped his hand when Regina caught up with him, and he realised she could have magicked a bandage, or magicked a healed hand. Could he do it himself? 'Heal,' he said. Nothing happened. 'Seat,' he said, pointing before him. Nothing. He gave a chuckle, and turned to Regina. 'Can you make a seat for us, Gina?'

Regina made a garden seat within an opalescent bower of glaced heroin. Around it she modelled a garden, its trees threading up into dappled detail. They sat down, with earth stars at their feet.

'Whatever it was,' Leo laughed, 'I think I burnt it out already.'

Leo felt light and electrified since his spawning of the moon. For a moment he had found himself unnaturally translated. But in the midst of it, he was reminded of his own real power. His soul was arched like an eyebrow, drawn like a bow. He had whole worlds up his sleeve. He anticipated his future with a brilliance of feeling.

'I confess your world can be beautiful, Gina. But I can only implement absurdities in it. What use is freedom here?'

'I am free to love you and think of you off and on without end.'

Leo was glad he no longer made her feel awkward, but apparently he could not help but often make her sad.

'What will you do?' she asked.

'I will live in the past, the present and the future. Justice to all three shall strive within me. Jagged and his octopus have a time machine. Come with me, Gina.'

'Back to the world that made you so angry?'

'I had every reason to be ... I had reason to protest, Gina. Since then countless revolutions have tanked, apparently. And law is weak, inert – it only moves and seems alive when thrust aside. When nothing is just, what difference whether anyone is spared? Pain is so near itself it can't know anything else. So is the happiness of constant fortune.'

'So?'

Leo reddened. The idea had seemed important. It *was* important. He carried his own criteria for value like a geiger counter and invariably upon detecting something of merit, onlookers' dismay confirmed his judgement. Now it reassured him to find his beliefs were so resilient.

'And besides,' Regina continued, 'my Uncle, the

Duke, would miss me terribly. That reminds me.' She drew a golden scimitar from empty air. It was the 'sacraface' sword from the Duke's party, sheathed in belted leather. 'He wanted you to have this, in thanks for making his performance such a success. He said he believed you were a ... a "sword saint"?'

'I don't know what that is. But it's very kind of him.' He took the sword and stood, strapping it over his shoulder.

A snail with a back like a bannister curve sped by.

'Is it true, Leo.'

'What.'

'That nothing here can mean anything.'

'Yes, it's true.'

'You've cursed me. Yes, that's the word. Cursed.'

'I didn't mean to. It's just the truth. Come with me.'

She looked at the ground.

He strode away from their strange arbor.

Leo was a long way off when she called after him. 'It was the dream! I gave you a ring! We did it together!'

THE LAST MAN

Showing By What Means Leo Would Depart

Principal Krill sat on his glass-bottomed beach, looking at the twist of carnival ride which ornamented the shallows to the right, a looped silhouette against the salmon sky. He watched fish dart beneath the transparent pane upon which his track-mounted vat was stood. Amid lush dendritic seaweed and floating particles like green snow moved a fish like a blossom of iridescent spikes; a fish like a padlock of glossy jelly; a fish like a human head with cat's ears for fins. Another looked like a block and tackle made of satin, yet another like a tumbleweed of thorny bones. Was his scene authentic? Large numbers of fish were called 'schools', but what did they teach? He watched the pattern of their movements carefully, trying to learn. Could his own creations teach him anything he didn't already know?

Along the long clear pane strode Leo del Toro, his purple leather coat flapping broadly. 'Hey, balloon-head – how are the nozzles?'

'Yes, indeed. I'm sure such repartee plays beautifully where you're going. Your visit here has been attended by many inconveniences – but has been instructive, I think?'

Leo stopped. 'How do you know I'm going? Does Jagged know?'

'Even he can guess. A brain that tops out at around mediocre, but a good man.'

'He seems quite smart to me.'

'His understanding goes deep, but only in one location. It's the same with many people. Specialists in their own belief.'

Leo looked around at the beach littered with machine cogs the size of castles. Krill let the silence be, a while, his anatomy ever furling and re-furling. Beneath Leo's boots were freckled stones, magnified by clear water. A short distance away moved a crab in a binding of Moroccan suede. It was nipped at by an advance arm of the tide, but continued on its way.

'The equational surface of the situation is misleading,' Krill suggested. 'You know the notion of freedom can be mapped over anything – that doesn't make it so. I have an urge to leave, myself.'

'It's all the same to me.'

Krill's head shifted, bulbing against his jar. 'A theory: time is a habit, super-imposed upon one of the less visible dimensions. It would appear that all the vertices in the universe couldn't help you escape it. But it's a habit that comes as one of the conditions of being alive. Thankfully, we start gasping our life out from the moment we're landed. Nature is gradual, but not reluctant.'

'A human being is an anchor of meat, I know the theory. That how your time machine works? By making people dead?'

Krill released a flurry of glooping bubbles, his

version of dismissive laughter. 'You'll find it interesting. You'll be encapsulated during the journey. Atomic suspension – it's the same way I allow damp and dust to co-exist in my labs. In case of emergency, the brain can be jettisoned. You probably won't need it, in the Twenty-First. Have your beliefs ready for inspection. And you'll be cemetery soup before anyone thanks you. Remember that.'

'Why?'

'Time is large. The forces of evil win out, finally, across several angles. The forces of good win out, finally, across several others. A billion or more other forces win out, finally, across yet more.'

'The forces of oppression depend on our comforting ourselves with those sorts of interpretations, rather than actually doing anything. You make me sick, squid.' Leo made to go.

'As someone who's seen a beach, then,' Krill asked quickly, 'what do you think this one needs?'

'Other than a non-transparent surface?'

Startled, Krill bluffed it. 'Of course.'

Leo considered a while. 'Tar,' he said. 'Tar and its smell makes a real beach.' He walked away, calling back. 'And get rid of those rollercoasters or whatever they're meant to be.'

When they parted, neither had said anything which deeply surprised the other, and nothing was decided which had not already been decided.

Krill watched the tide's stretching suds. 'If that's a beach, I'm not sure I care for it. But, real is real.'

Leo climbed a dirt path up a steep bluff and crossed

a metal suspension bridge, its guywires gossiping as he crossed. Jagged stood waiting in the trapezoid doorway to Krill's acid-green-flake observatory. He smiled and greeted Leo without a trace of rancour. 'Our sorties and culminations reach an end. Come in.'

A house with portholes, thought Leo. *Cool.* He followed Lord Jagged down a stairwell crowded on either side with cupboards and bookshelves. He saw maps and pictures hung on pegs, empty jars and pints of dead gold. Leo was feeling unsteady, his legs repeatedly tensing with causeless vertigo. Was the proximity of the time machine already affecting him?

Jagged stopped him and pointed to a broad window which looked out on the beach. 'I've told them you are going.'

Along the glassy strand moved a heartbreak parade of harlequins and minotaurs, luminists and princes, queens and pipers. Here was Argonheart Po, Pastor Bulbous, Sweet Orb Mace, Gaf the Horse in Tears, O'Kala Incarnadine, the Luton Clown and the Earl of Carbolic. The Iron Orchid floated forth like a parade float, dressed in a spotless silver robe and holding a trident. Profumo the Monkey capered and bobbed, belching smoke. My Lady Charlotina was grabbing fistfuls of priests' ears from a basket and flinging them like wedding rice. A big man with a head like a baby's set with a cyclops eye was followed by the sharp-featured Volospion, pale even to the lips, his eyes gleaming like a bug's rump. Jherek Carnelian strode along in a glowing white tuxedo and the octopal Krill followed after in his dozer.

Falcomatis of the Jet Black Trauma Feathers was rezed in the livery of an exhausted Saxon. Werther was there, ghostly as a watermark. Mistress Christia the Everlasting Concubine reclined in a furlined sled being drawn by Baron Coma, whose head was now a back-curving scapula of iron bars. Roxanne Ansari tilted in a bottle-green pyrex cone, her hat a square-ish funnel into which she was dropping lit coals. When she smiled, licks of flame swam out between her teeth. Again the Shuttle Clue was a barrel-bellied bear of cobalt velvet, playing a neon glockenspiel. Bishop Castle's crenellated crown and candy crook swayed above the gaudy demonstration of dazzling jewelled turbans, random pageantry, venom yellow masks and morphing gowns and tunics. Beyond them waves folded together, detailed as fingerprints.

And this patterned pandemonium proceeded in an endlessly intricate dance, keeping time to different rises of the song, swapping their lefts and rights, circling and prancing and merging all through one-another. Whisper Terrible hopped like a sparrow, his tail feathers clicking together like tin templates, carrying with him as barometric treasure a miniature immensity of slow warm golden snow. Even the obsessive buccaneer Fox Grave was there. Only Regina Sparks seemed to be absent. The procession was berry-bright as a burning billion-colour postcard, in which Leo saw all the new colours of olvis, cry, zild and severin. And every mouth was singing:

Tears and a voyage, fiercest friend
Go your way in joy and rage

Remember us and keep our secret
In your strange and fearful age

At the simplicity of their cartoonlike, breathless life, he found himself waving like a child.

'Think of us this way,' said Jagged softly. 'As actors, spirits that will melt into air. Let's go below, to the time lens.'

Leaving the carnivalesque scene behind, they passed a door through which Leo glimpsed a sort of library with a world globe, and continued their descent, arriving at a pair of hammered wulfenite doors. Jagged pushed through these and Leo followed into a purple marble chamber decked in fitted fluorite. Standing upright without visible support was a thin hoop of silver the size of a garage door. 'Is that it?' Leo asked.

Jagged was scrutinising a set of chrome controls upholstered in butterscotch leather. 'It's a transphotic lens. A layered valve of mercury flowing in contrary spirals. While moving a little from side-to-side each second, it spins upon the axis it will have one second in the future and one second in the past. Think about that. The effect is known as Cumulative Implication. You'll travel parallel to events. Not invisible exactly, just one second oblique to it all. It's called demitime. An envelope which is proof against interference during the trip.' A couple of toroidal cylinders started to crackle with contained lightning.

Leo was distracted by a small observation bubble that looked out on an ocean in which living Christmas decorations celebrated strangely.

'You're making it up, right?' he whispered.

On a narrow pedestal was something like a molecule model.

'What's this?'

'A map – an open-work cosmos of wireframe eternities.' He saw Leo's dubious look, and smiled. 'I don't understand it all, Leo. I suspect it is a puzzle unintelligible to any but the infinitely humorous.' He pointed. 'There's your conveyance.'

'Rocinante!' In delight Leo approached the motorbike propped in the corner. It was only when he drew near that he realised the disc brakes were immense pearl sections and the headlamp was a giant sapphire. The frame appeared to be a single twist of solid diamond cradling a massive habit of carnallite.

'Here's where the original came in.' Jagged indicated the floor. A greenish tyre-mark went from the lens ramp to the near wall, which bore a fragmented cavity. 'And there's where you hit the wall upon arrival,' he said, 'knocking yourself out. We gave you a translation pill and set you going again a few miles from here. I don't know how much you remember. You'll find the so-called fabric of time rather rough. It'll be pulled right through you like a conjuror's cloth.'

Leo swung onto the bike.

'Remember,' Jagged continued, 'the Morphail Theory states that nobody can remain for long in a past where they don't belong. When someone travels forward as you have, the chronoverse generally considers the traveller to then belong in the forward time. This is why you may well bounce all the way back here to the End. One thing you can do to help prevent it is to be as inconspicuous as possible. Don't try to change or effect anything and time will tolerate you. Go with the flow, or you'll be spat out.'

'I don't think I can guarantee it.'

Jagged returned to the control bank and eyed a round amber screen. 'I've set you to go rather further back than your own time and then bounce forward to the target year – this may increase your chances of staying put when you land.'

'Overstretching the elastic.'

'Something like that. It may on the other hand send you back here all the faster, with your eyes shaken to blood. It's a precision instrument only as far as we can prove.'

'No harm in being certain, Jagged – if you're right.'

'The same goes for you, del Toro. In any case I'll study my records closely. If I find your frown amid some historical crowd after your supposed disappearance, I'll know you arrived safely.'

'Then what? Will you try it yourself?'

Busying himself with the controls, Jagged did not look at him. 'Oh, you know, I'm rather a busy man.'

At the turn of a switch the empty hoop filled with a photovoltaic translucence which crackled and banged as fluctuations scrambled across its surface. A windstorm was blasting through the chamber. Astride his bike, Leo already felt a glutinous suction toward the viscous disk. He turned to Jagged with a nervous smile.

Jagged gestured at the roiling time lens, his puffy

lilac sleeves rippling, and shouted above the roar. 'There's the door from this cooling planet to your antique land! It'll look rather dull at first when you arrive! You have fewer colours back there! May time deny thee glory and grant thee peace!'

'I thank you for your time and efforts!'

Leo kicked off and surged up the ramp. Regina Sparks burst into the room and leapt onto the bike, clutching her arms around Leo and flinching against his back as they passed through the blazing surface and howled down the throat of time.

As Jagged watched, their phosphene after-image rippled as though liquefacted, and disappeared.

18

THE WORLD

What Moving Spectacles Befell Our Travellers
Upon Their Voyage

The room shrivelled behind them and with a sense of massive acceleration they were wailing through blurred mottlings of rushing matter. The sensation of falling was disconcerting, as if they were dropping down the eye of a twister. Leo, Regina and the gemstone bike were glossed in an encapsulating film of timestuff, a bubble in the flow of time. A glance ahead made it clear they were following lashing lines of force, a rollercoaster ride through roaring eternity. Angled avenues opened in midair, conjuring new distances. Leo could see societies which, like his own, were derelict but inhabited. Then other states, their cosmologies spreading like blastoma. All at a distance beyond the rushing colloidal wall of the swerving contraflow. Leo became sensible of confused noises in the air, incoherent sounds of anger and regret; bland dishonesty and accusation. Every instant opened voluminously, pouring in at every avenue of sense. Transfinite scenes arced through the time travellers, vivid moments in progress.

Leo and Regina witnessed the many instants that catastrophes were set off by the clutching mediocre. They saw discovered knowledge ignored for millennia until fashion's schedule decreed it could be acknowledged. They glimpsed erstwhile guardians who slumbered through slavery, legislators coining liberties with the implied right to withhold them, and always a majority willing to submit to whatever was stamped with the local logo of authority. Muted lives in their billions, unconscious even of their fear. Billions who saw rebellion in buying something different. Whole populations swept away like fireplace ashes.

These scenes presented themselves like glimpses on a journey, but charged with every angle of significance and each iteration of their context in time. Here were incoherent clashes in roads and fields, massacres without drama or remembrance. Animals treated as failed prototypes, women as precocious peripherals or mysteries to worship and men as worth no more than their earnings. Umbrella masses crowded down a street like huge black barnacles. Residents rattled like graveyard storage. The poor betrayed one another in a crisscross of accusations, an automated scourge set off by law to run its course. Those who asked only to be allowed to build their own limits were forced to expiate their innocence through complicity in war. With each stop-off, Leo felt as if he had let his mind wander and it had become snagged briefly on someone else's life. Here was dreary malice and the depressing blazonry of empire. Temples of prejudice and schools of hysteria, every textbook a funeral mass for an idea. It was dismal and grotesque, never cinematic or compelling. While good men cocooned by limited experience spoke more generously of humanity than was wise: 'It would be ridiculous to berate an organised institution like the government for a lack of humanity and yet that is, after all, the problem.' Leo and Regina saw moments constructed entirely of reversals, others of so much denial humanity almost became the shabby robot race it aspired to. Humanity's choices were so scrupulously bad at every stage that it seemed these could not have been selected by chance or accident; their sabotages so intricate, they could not have been performed absent-mindedly. Good sense was never the default position – fear was. Fear filled reason's ocean with predators. Plans were made, needless of secrecy or intrigue. 'The power to make laws is antiseptic against justice. The closed symmetry of injustice is preferred to the ventilative release of justice because the former lasts longer.' Leo did not know if it was the sense of eternally falling or the lacerative endlessness of history's conditions that were making him sick. They were passing over wounds a century wide.

At times the time travellers swerved askew through people's bioluminescent innards, vaulted gulfs of eerie absence or were rocked by galvanic blasts of intersection, but their headlong flight through the writhing tunnel of quantum foam showed no signs of ending. They were treated to contentless optimism as a check on empathy, fear and its cresting chaos of decrees, the auctioning of the thoughts of great men to causes they didn't suit, and the denial that the deepest level of want's gravity-well is inescapable irrespective of invention or effort. They saw all brands of cruelty – negligent, unstinting, habitual, automated

– but it seemed they did not journey back far enough to witness the pioneering. Between each phase of more sophisticated cruelty humanity lapsed back to its savage starter position, but beyond a certain point, in this matter as in everything else, the time travellers found a complete absence of meaningful novelty.

Both Leo and Regina realised they were no longer looking at the details of the scenes presented to them. The passing components were blurring into patterns, resolving into continuous waves of delirious repetition. The tidemarks of recorded history were blanded and ignored, wave after wave the same forms, changing only in scale and detail. Every circumstance erased in a wave of usurpation could be recognised again in later ages, the same gestalts retaining the same flavours through all time. The disregard or ignorance of previous wisdom was continually visible as pulsing ghost washes of amnesia. Leo recognised such historical cycles were not circular but spherical, a design allowing for those spirals of variation that hid the pattern from close observers.

Plunging through this infinite regress of recoiling patterns, the time-sick couple were unaware they were periodically screaming and letting forth yelps of an extrahuman quality. Nerve bursts of deceleration signalled a new vision and they were spectating a courtroom through a wall of light crawling with hooks. The crime was an act of violence in the wrong direction, upward against the grain of hierarchy, and was thus being declared an especial abomination. There was a sickening falsity to the process as those present denied the obverse armatures behind it. Leo was familiar with the artificial obtuseness of court process. One atom of truth would wreck this farce. But truth was occluded behind an invisible barrier, like the very one separating Leo and Regina from the scene. Leo shouted the power differential at the jury – one juror glanced quizzically in his direction for a moment. Both Leo and Regina yelled at once, and several people turned their way, frowning – but this anomaly quickly healed over. Was it Time itself resisting interference, or human nature, or both? Perhaps Leo and Regina were as socially invisible as top-down violence – the unremarkable, non-abominable kind. Before Leo could attempt to physically effort through the barrier, the scene unstitched and they were speeding on again. Waves of coloured elements boiled past them, seemingly inset with ductile windows and silver beads the size of footballs. There was a pause to glimpse a brief moment of torture never named or reported, which dropped away like an elevator as the trip reversed, sucking them in the opposite direction. They were catapulted backward through themselves, trailing biophotons.

They saw now only the swipes and lattices of history and were nauseated by this endlessly transitional space. Then once again the air was filled with phantoms, born with office eyes and office brains. Scenes flashed through. They were near Leo's own time. He recognised the chanted creed of state selfhood groups: '1. We admit we are powerless under the State – that our lives are managed. 2. We believe that a power greater than ourselves will choose to keep us safe. 3. We have made a decision to turn our will and our lives over to the care of the State.'

Boundaries were interacting with his body and the twisting tunnel seemed less substantial, bangs of collision warping its surface. Smoke cleared to reveal a younger version of himself crouching against a shattered storefront during the HR1955 Riots, talking to a vlogger as he superglued a neck wound. '... with or without the government.'

'What's wrong with a government?'

'Well at the very least I have to get some scouts behind it or it's a blind spot.'

A loud explosion threw the scene behind them as they plunged onward, then the centrifugal force spun down and the streaming ribbons of time's long track ceased in mid-air. The motorcycle and its riders emerged three feet above the ground and screeched to earth in a dark alley where it crashed into a crowd of trashcans.

The past was chill. The only witness in the alley was a homeless guy trying to light a dead cigarette off a memory stick. Frozen in the act, he stared at them like a lemur. Regina inspected a trashcan, its ridged metal grey as flint, and as cold. She raised her head, trying to sense beyond the dark air. 'Lightning bends along the walls here in sort of rubber veins, doesn't it?'

'Yes,' said Leo, standing off of the bike. His time was already percolating into her. Leo feared for her blue swimming pool heart. 'You'd better put a top on.'

Regina turned a power ring. Nothing happened. 'Oh. Of course.'

Leo removed the scabbard of his sword, took off his coat, gave it to Regina, and replaced the sword.

'The things we saw ... from the tunnel.' Regina was shivering despite the coat. 'Such things do not happen at the End of Time. Why come to Denial?'

Leo sighed. 'All right, let's call it Denial – a society in which everything is priced. A rose made of tickets.' He thought about how to explain it. 'When times change and fashion turns, people deny that they were ever there, in the past fashion. When a holocaust ends and fashion turns, people deny that they were ever there, tolerating that horror. Even if such a thing is not happening at this moment, people are people. Only as a last resort do people dissent, and then rarely. This requires an awakening. I'm more certain than ever that an injustice doesn't cease just because it's in the past and forgotten. It exists until it's remedied, or at the very least honestly acknowledged.'

Leo retrieved the diamond from the pocket of his coat – the one he had found in his boot. He walked over and gave it to the man in the alley, explaining what it was. As he returned to Regina she frowned at him. 'If things are so bad,' she asked, 'how can such a gesture make a difference?'

'It might make a difference to him. Come on, we need to set up.'

Leo righted the bike, climbed on and gestured for her to join him.

'The larger world of life,' said Regina to herself, the other half of something clicking together in her mind, 'came from the hope in the smallest space.' She swung on and they started into the night.

'Everyone else is pretending,' Leo said. 'Let's behave as though for us the uncut pages of history are blank.'

'Did they have any effect?' asked the octopal Krill in the humming purple time room. 'Have they upset the timestream?'

Jagged consulted the chrono-controls. 'There's no sign of it. Nothing's been altered.'

Some fluctuant motion crossed Krill's face. Jagged observed him with concern. 'What's your decision, pulsatile friend?'

Krill excitedly fluttered the blue-grey petals of his underside. 'I'm jumping into the stream. Decant me somewhere quiet and deep. Somewhere I won't be obliged to offer advice.'

'There's every chance you'll land in a frying pan, but people would be startled if you offered remarks about it. Echo them in a wretched, bewildered tone and they'll be happy.'

Distoles and cistoles were gapping in Krill's bulbous head, sending thoughtful bubble trails aloft in his vat. 'Dawn Ages, isn't it? Broadest nature, at least, was beyond the scope of their authority.'

'For a while, at least. And what if you don't return?'

'I don't intend to, providing I splash down with accuracy. Morphail's researches are promising – his devices may well be more stable than mine. He'll carry you, old fellow. And in ancient waters murky as potion, I'll be a plague upon suction eels. Farewell.'

Without another word, Krill backed around and tracked his vehicular jar toward the lens platform.

The portal ignited, whirling with blue liquid fire as he rolled up the short ramp. Jagged glimpsed a black infinity of contours around the departing form and the silhouette deliquesced. Krill was gone into the raw past.

Jagged left the silent dome and walked into the glittering present. In the valleys and skies his friends were already brewing new effects and affectations. For a while everyone would be taken with the notion of flags and enjoy designing their own. This would be the only legacy of the del Toro affair to last for any length of time – this and Doctor Volospion's reduction in sarcasm, which he accomplished by means of a power ring. 'I could always reverse it,' he would tell Lord Jagged, 'if I encounter anyone who might be improved by a downpour of bile.' But he never did.

Now Jagged arrived at Castle Canaria, thinking about his departed colleagues. He stopped on the front path, stooping to pick a celandine for his buttonhole. Satisfied, he proceeded inside, passing under the arched inscription written in Olmec Japanese: SAVE THE HEART